THE RIDDLE OF THE THIRD MILE

Colin Dexter

BANTAM BOOKS
TORONTO · NEW YORK · LONDON · SYDNEY · AUCKLAND

This edition contains the complete text
of the original hardcover edition.
NOT ONE WORD HAS BEEN OMITTED.

THE RIDDLE OF THE THIRD MILE

*A Bantam Book / published by arrangement with
St. Martin's Press*

PRINTING HISTORY

St. Martin's edition published February 1984

Bantam edition / June 1988

ISBN 0-553-27363-9

Published simultaneously in the United States and Canada

---

*Bantam Books are published by Bantam Books, a division of Bantam
Doubleday Dell Publishing Group, Inc. Its trademark, consisting of
the words "Bantam Books" and the portrayal of a rooster, is Regis-
tered in U.S. Patent and Trademark Office and in other countries.
Marca Registrada. Bantam Books, 666 Fifth Avenue, New York, New
York 10103*

PRINTED IN THE UNITED STATES OF AMERICA

O   9 8 7 6 5 4 3 2 1

For my daughter, Sally

And whosoever shall compel thee to go a mile, go with him twain.

St. Matthew 5, 41

THE
FIRST
MILE

CHAPTER ONE

Monday, 7th July

In which a veteran of the El Alamein offensive finds cause to recall the most tragic day of his life.

There had been the three of them—the three Gilbert brothers: the twins, Alfred and Albert; and the younger boy, John, who had been killed one day in North Africa. And it was upon his dead brother that the thoughts of Albert Gilbert were concentrated as he sat alone in a North London pub just before closing-time: John, who had always been less sturdy, more vulnerable, than the formidable, inseparable, and virtually indistinguishable pair known to their schoolmates as "Alf 'n Bert"; John, whom his elder brothers had always sought to protect; the same John whom they had not been able to protect that terrible day in 1942.

It was in the early morning of 2nd November that "Operation Supercharge" had been launched against the Rahman Track to the west of El Alamein. To Gilbert, it had always seemed strange that this campaign was considered by war historians to be such a miraculous triumph of strategic planning, since from his brief but not unheroic participation in that battle he could remember only the blinding confusions around him during that pre-dawn attack. "The tanks must go through" had been the previous evening's orders, filtered down from the red-tabbed hierarchy of Armoured Brigade to the field-officers and the NCOs of the Royal Wiltshires, into which regiment Alf and

Bert had enlisted in October 1939, soon to find themselves grinding over Salisbury Plain in the drivers' seats of antique tanks—both duly promoted to full corporals, and both shipped off to Cairo at the end of 1941. And it had been a happy day for the two of them when brother John had joined them in mid-1942, as each side built up reinforcements for the imminent show-down.

On that morning of 2nd November, at 0105 hours, Alf and Bert moved their tanks forward along the north side of Kidney Ridge, where they came under heavy fire from the German 88s and the Panzers dug in at Tel Aqqaqir. The guns of the Wiltshires' tanks had spat and belched their shells into the enemy lines, and the battle raged furiously. But it was an uneven fight, for the advancing British tanks were open targets for the anti-tank weapons and, as they nosed forward, they were picked off piecemeal from the German emplacements.

It was a hard and bitter memory, even now; but Gilbert allowed his thoughts full rein. He could do so now. Yes, and it was important that he *should* do so.

About fifty yards ahead of him, one of the leading tanks was burning, the commander's body sprawled across the hatch, the left arm dangling down towards the main turret, the tin-helmeted head spattered with blood. Another tank, to his left, lurched to a crazy standstill as a German shell shattered its left-side track, four men jumping down and sprinting back towards the comparative safety of the boundless, anonymous sands behind them.

The noise of battle was deafening as shrapnel soared and whistled and plunged and dealt its death amidst the desert in that semi-dawn. Men shouted and pleaded and ran—and died; some blessedly swiftly in an instantaneous annihilation, others lingeringly as they lay mortally wounded on the bloody sand. Yet others burned to death inside their tanks as the twisted metal of the hatches jammed, or shot-up limbs could find no final, desperate leverage.

Then it was the turn of the tank immediately to Gilbert's right—an officer leaping down, clutching a hand that spurted blood, and just managing to race clear before the tank exploded into blinding flame.

Gilbert's turret-gunner was shouting down to him.

"Christ! See that, Bert? No wonder they christened these fuckin' things 'Tommycookers'!"

"You just keep giving it to the bastards, Wilf!" Gilbert had shouted back.

But he received no reply, for Wilfred Barnes, Private in the Royal Wiltshire Yeomanry, had spoken his last words.

The next thing Gilbert saw was the face of Private Phillips as the latter wrestled with the driver's hatch and helped him out.

"Run like hell, corporal! The other two have had it."

They had struggled only some forty yards before flinging themselves down as another shell kicked up the sand just ahead of them, spewing its steel fragments in a shower of jagged metal. And when Gilbert finally looked up, he found that Private Phillips, too, was dead—a lump of twisted steel embedded in his lower back. For several minutes after that, Gilbert sat where he was, severely shocked but apparently uninjured. His eyes looked down at his legs, then at his arms; he felt his face and his chest; then he tried to wriggle his toes in his army boots. Just thirty seconds ago there had been four men. And now there was only one— *him*. His first conscious thought (which he could recall so vividly) was a feeling of ineffable anger; but almost immediately his heart rejoiced as he saw a fresh wave of 8th Armoured Brigade tanks moving up through the gaps between the broken or blazing hulks of the first assault formation. Only gradually did a sense of vast relief surge through him—relief that he had survived, and he said a brief prayer to his God in gratitude for coming through.

Then he heard the voice.

"For Christ's sake, get out of here, corporal!" It was the officer with the bleeding hand, a lieutenant in the Wiltshires—a man who was known as a stickler for discipline, and a bit pompous with it; but not an unpopular officer, and indeed the one who the night before had relayed to his men the Montgomery memorandum.

"You a'right, sir?" Gilbert asked.

"Not too bad." He looked down at his hand, the right index finger hanging only by a tissue of flesh to the rest of his hand. "What about you?"

"I'm fine, sir."

"We'll get back to Kidney Ridge—that's about all we *can* do." Even here, amid the horrifying scenes of carnage, the voice was that of a pre-war wireless announcer, clipped and precise—what they called an "Oxford" accent.

The two men scrambled through the soft sand for a few hundred yards before Gilbert collapsed.

"Come *on*! What's the matter with you, man?"

"I dunno, sir. I just don't seem. . . ." He looked down at his left trouser-leg, where he had felt the fire of some intense pain; and he saw that blood had oozed copiously through the rough khaki. Then he put his left hand to the back of his leg and felt the sticky morass of bleeding flesh where half his calf had been shot away. He grinned ruefully:

"You go on, sir. I'll bring up the rear."

But already the focus had changed. A tank which had seemed to be bearing down upon them suddenly slewed round upon its tracks so that now it faced backwards, its top completely sheared away. Its engine, however, still throbbed and growled, the gears grinding like the gnashing of tortured teeth in hell. But Gilbert heard more than that. He heard the voice of a man crying out in the agony of some God-forsaken despair, and he found himself staggering towards the tank as it lurched round yet again in a spurting spray of sand. The man in the driver's seat was alive! Thereafter Gilbert forgot himself completely: forgot his leg-wound, forgot his fear, forgot his relief, forgot his anger. He thought only of Private Phillips from Devizes. . . .

The hatch was a shattered weld of hot steel that just would not open—not yet. *Almost* it came; and the sweat showered down Gilbert's face as he swore and wrenched and whimpered at his task. The petrol-tank ignited with a soft, almost apologetic "whush," and Gilbert knew it was a matter only of seconds before another man was doomed to death inside a Tommycooker.

"For Chrissake!" he yelled to the officer behind him. "Help! Please! I've—nearly—" He wrenched for the last time at the hatch, and the sweat poured again on to his bulging, vein-ridged forearms.

"Can't you fuckin' well see? Can't you—" His voice tailed off in desperation, and he fell to the sand, overwhelmed by failure and exhaustion.

"Leave it, corporal! Come away! That's an *order*!"

So Gilbert crawled away across the sand and wept in frenetic despair, his grimed face looking up to see through his tears the glaze in the officer's eyes . . . the glaze of frozen cowardice. But he remembered little else except the screaming of that burning fellow soldier. And it was only later that he thought he'd recognized the voice—for he hadn't seen the face.

He was picked up (so they told him) soon after this by an army truck, and the next thing he could remember was lying comfortably in very white sheets and red blankets in a military hospital. They didn't tell him until two weeks later that his brother John, tank-driver with the 8th Armoured Brigade, had been killed in the second-phase offensive.

Then Albert Gilbert had been almost sure; but even now, he wasn't *quite* sure. He knew one thing, though, for nothing could erase from his cerebral cortex the name of the officer who, one morning in the desert, in the battle for the ridge at Tel El Aqqaqir, had been tried in the balance of courage—and been found wanting. Lieutenant Browne-Smith, that was the name. Funny name, really, with an "e" in the middle. A name he'd never seen again, until recently.

Until very recently indeed.

CHAPTER TWO

Wednesday, 9th July

We are in the University of Oxford, at the marks-meeting of the seven examiners appointed for "Greats."

"He would have walked a first otherwise," said the Chairman. He looked down again at the six separate assessments, all of them liberally sprinkled with alphas and beta plusses except for the one opposite Greek History, where stood a feeble-looking beta double minus/delta. Not, this last, the category of the finest minds.

"Well, what do you think, gentlemen? Worth a viva, surely, isn't he?"

With minimal effort, five of the other six men, seated at a large table bestrewn with scripts and lists and mark-sheets, raised the palms of their hands in agreement.

"*You* don't think so?" The Chairman had turned towards the seventh member of the examining panel.

"No, Chairman. He's not worth it—not on this evidence." He flicked the script in front of him. "He's proved quite conclusively to me that he knows next to nothing outside fifth-century Athens. I'm sorry. If he wanted a first, he ought to have done a bit more work than *this*." Again he flicked the script, an expression of disgust further disfiguring a face that had probably been sour from birth. Yet, as all those present knew, no one else in the University could award a delicate grading like B+/B+?+ with such confident aplomb, or justify it with such fierce conviction.

"We all know, though, don't we" (it was one of the other members), "that sometimes it's a bit hit-and-miss, the questions we set, I mean—especially in Greek History."

"I set the questions," interrupted the dissident, with some heat. "There's never been a fairer spread."

The Chairman looked very tired. "Gentlemen. We've had a long, hard day, and we're almost at the finishing-post. Let's just—"

"Of course he's worth a viva," said one of the others with a quiet, clinching authority. "I marked his Logic paper—it's brilliant in places."

"I'm sure you're right," said the Chairman. "We fully take your point about the history paper, Dr. Browne-Smith, but . . ."

"So be it—you're the Chairman."

"Yes, you're quite right. I *am* the Chairman and this man's going to get his viva!"

It was a nasty little exchange, and the Logic examiner immediately stepped in with a peace proposal. "Perhaps, Dr. Browne-Smith, you might agree to viva him yourself?"

But Browne-Smith shook his aching head. "No! I'm biased against the fellow—and all this marking—it's been quite enough for me. I'm doing nothing else."

The Chairman, too, was anxious to end the meeting on a happier note: "What about asking Andrews? Would *he* be prepared to take it on?"

Browne-Smith shrugged. "He's quite a good young man."

So the Chairman wrote his final note: "To be viva-ed by Mr. Andrews (Lonsdale), 18th July"; and the others began to collect their papers together.

"Well, thank you all very much, gentlemen. Before we finish, though, can we just think about our final meeting? Almost certainly it's got to be Wednesday 23rd or Thursday 24th."

Browne-Smith was the only one of the panel who hadn't taken out his diary; and when the meeting was finally fixed for 10 a.m. on Wednesday the 23rd, he appeared to take no notice whatsoever.

The Chairman had observed this. "All right with you, Dr. Browne-Smith?"

"I was just about to say, Chairman, that I'm afraid I probably shan't be with you for the final meeting. I should very much like to be, of course, but I—I've got to be. . . . Well, I probably shan't be in Oxford."

The Chairman nodded a vague, uneasy understanding. "Well, we'll try to do our best without you. Thank you, anyway, for all the help you've been—as ever." He closed the thick, black volume in front of him, and looked at his wristwatch: 8:35 p.m. Yes, it had been a long, hard day. No wonder, perhaps, that he'd become a little snappy at the end.

Six members of the panel agreed to repair to the King's Arms in Broad Street; but the seventh member, Dr. Browne-Smith, begged leave to be excused. Instead, he left the Examination Schools, walked slowly along The High, and let himself through the back-door ("Senior Fellows Only") into Lonsdale College. Once in his rooms, he swallowed six Paracetamol tablets, and lay down fully-clothed upon his bed, where for the next hour his brain blundered around uncontrollably in his head. Then he fell asleep.

On the morning of the next day, Thursday, 10th July, he received a letter. A very strange and rather exciting letter.

CHAPTER THREE

Friday, 11th July

In which we learn of an Oxford don's invitation to view the vice and viciousness of life in a notorious area of the metropolis.

Never throughout his life—almost sixty-seven years of it now—had Oliver Maximilian Alexander Browne-Smith (with an "e" and with hyphenation), MC, MA, D. Phil., really come to terms with his inordinately ponderous names. Predictably, in his prep-school days he had been nicknamed "Omar"; and now, with only one year before his University appointment was due to be statutorily terminated, he knew that amongst the undergraduates he had acquired the opprobrious sobriquet of "Malaria," which was not so predictable and very much nastier.

It was some small surprise to him, therefore, to find how quickly he had managed to bring himself to terms, in a period of only a few weeks, with the fact that he would quite certainly be dead well within a twelvemonth ("At the very outside, since you insist on the truth, Dr. Browne-Smith"). What he did not realize, however, as he walked on to Platform One at Oxford Station, was that he would be dead within a shorter period than that so confidently predicted by his distinguished and expensive consultant.

A very much shorter period.

As he made his way to the rear end of the platform, he kept his eyes lowered, and looked with distaste at the empty beer-cans and litter that bestrewed the "up" line. A

few of his University colleagues, some from Lonsdale, were
fairly frequent passengers on the 9:12 a.m. train from Oxford to Paddington, and the truth was that he felt no wish to
converse with any of them. Under his left arm he held a
copy of *The Times*, just purchased from the station book-
stall; and in his right hand he held a brown leather briefcase. For a fine, bright morning in mid-July, it was
surprisingly chilly.

The yellow-fronted diesel snaked its slow way punc-
tually through the points just north of the station, and two
minutes later he was seated opposite a young couple in a
non-smoking compartment. Although an inveterate and incurable smoker himself, one who had dragged his wheezing
lungs through cigarettes at the rate of forty-plus a day for
fifty years, he had decided to impose upon himself some
token abstinence during the hour-long journey that lay
ahead of him. It seemed, somehow, appropriate. When the
train moved out, he folded *The Times* over and started on
the crossword, his mind registering nothing at all on the
first three of the clues across. But on the fourth, a hint of a
grin formed around his slightly lopsided mouth as he looked
down again at the extraordinarily apposite words: "First
thing in Soho tourist's after? (8)." He quickly wrote in
"stripper"; and with more and more letters thenceforth
making their horizontal and vertical inroads into the di-
agram-grid, the puzzle was finished well before Reading.
Then, hoping that the couple opposite had duly noted his
cruciverbalistic competence—if not the ugly stump of his
right index finger, chopped off at the first joint—he leaned
back in his seat as far as his longish legs would allow, closed
his eyes, and concentrated his thoughts on the very strange
reason that was drawing him to London that day.

At Paddington he was almost the last person to leave
the train and, as he walked to the ticket-barrier, he saw that
it was still only 10:15 a.m. Plenty of time. He collected a
Paddington-Reading-Oxford timetable from the Information Bureau, bought a cup of coffee at the buffet, where he
lit a cigarette, and looked up the possible trains for his return journey. Curiously enough, he felt relaxed as he lit a
second cigarette from the first, and wondered vaguely what

times the pubs—and clubs—would be open in London. 11
a.m. perhaps? But that was a matter of no great moment.

It was 10:40 a.m. when he left the station buffet and
walked briskly to the Bakerloo line, where, as he queued
for his ticket, he realized that he must have left his timetable in the buffet. But that was of no great moment, either.
There were plenty of trains to choose from, and he'd made a
mental note of some of the times.

He could not have known, of course, that he would not
be travelling back to Oxford that night.

On the tube he opened his briefcase and took out two
sheets of paper: the first was a letter addressed to himself,
amateurishly typed but perfectly literate—a letter that still
seemed very strange to him; the second was a more professionally typed sheet (indeed, typed by Browne-Smith himself) comprising a list of students from Oxford University,
with the names of their colleges appended in brackets, and
the words "Class One, *Literae Humaniores*" printed across
the top in bold, red capitals. But Browne-Smith glanced
only cursorily at the two sheets through his bifocal lenses. It
appeared that he was merely reassuring himself that both
were still in existence. Nothing more.

At Edgware Road he looked up above the carriage-windows, noting that there were only two more stops, and for
almost the first time he felt a flutter of excitement somewhere in his diaphragm. It was that letter. . . . *Very* odd!
Even the address had been odd, with the full details carefully stated: Room 4, Staircase T, Second Quad, Lonsdale
College, Oxford. Such specificity was rare, and seemed to
suggest that whoever had sent the letter was more than usually anxious for it not to go astray—more than a little knowledgeable, too, about the college's geography . . . Staircase
T, Second Quad. . . . In his mind's eye, Browne-Smith saw
himself climbing those few stairs once more; climbing
them, as he had done for the past thirty years, up to the first
landing, where his own name, hand-printed in white,
Gothic lettering, still stood above the door. And immediately opposite him, Room 3—where George Westerby,
the Geography don, had lived for almost exactly the same
time: just one term longer than himself, in fact. Their mu-

tual hatred was intense, the whole college knew that,
though it might just have been different if Westerby had
ever been prepared to make the feeblest gesture towards
some reconciliation. But he had never done so.

Via the ziggurat of steep escalators, Browne-Smith
emerged at 11:05 a.m. into the bright sunlight of Piccadilly
Circus, crossed over into Shaftesbury Avenue, and immediately plunged into the maze of roads and alley-ways that
criss-cross the area off Great Windmill Street. Here
abounded small cinemas that featured films of hard, uncom-
promising porn, with stills outside of nudes and semi-
nudes, vast-breasted and voluptuous; clubs that promised
passers-by the prospects of erotic, non-stop nudity; bookshops that boasted the glossiest, grossest magazines for
paedophiles and buffs of bestiality. And it was along these
gaudy streets, beneath the orange and the yellow signs,
past the inviting doors, that Browne-Smith walked slowly,
savouring the uncensored atmosphere, and feeling himself
inexorably sucked into the cesspool that is known as Soho.

It was in a narrow lane just off Brewer Street that he
spotted it—as he'd known he would: "The Flamenco Topless Bar: No Membership Fee: Please Walk Straight
Down." The wide, shallow steps that led from the foyer
down to the subterranean premises had once been carpeted
in heavy crimson, but now the middle of the tread re-
sembled more the trampled sward of a National Trust
beauty-spot at the height of a glorious summer. He was
walking past, but there must have been some tell-tale hesitation in his step, for the acne-faced youth who lounged just
inside the doorway had spotted him already.

"Lovely girls in here, sir. Just walk straight down. No
membership fee."

"The bar is open, is it? I only want a drink."

"Bar's always open here, sir. Just walk straight down."
The young man stepped aside, and Browne-Smith took his
fateful step across the entrance and slowly descended to
The Flamenco Topless Bar. *Facilis descensus Averno.*

At the foot of the stairs further progress was barred by a
velvet drape, and he was wondering what he should do
when a seemingly disembodied head poked through a gap

in the middle of the curtain—the head of an attractive young girl of no more than nineteen or twenty years, the hazel eyes luridly blued and blackened by harsh mascaras, but the senuous mouth devoid of any lipstick. A pink tongue completed a slow circuit round the soft-looking mouth, and a pleasant voice asked simply and sweetly for only £1.

"There's no membership fee; it says so outside. And the man on the door said so."

The face smiled, as it always smiled at the gullible men who'd trodden those broad and easy stairs.

"It's not a membership fee—just admission. You know what I mean?" The eyes held his with simmering sexuality, and the note passed quickly through the crimson curtain.

The Flamenco Bar was a low-ceilinged affair with the seats grouped in *alcôves à deux*, towards one of which the young girl escorted him. She was, herself, fully clothed; and, after handing her client a buff-coloured drinks-list, she departed without a further word to her wonted seat behind a poor imitation of a drinking-man's bar, whereat she was soon deeply engrossed in her zodiacal predictions as reported in the *Daily Mirror*.

It seemed to Browne-Smith, as he struggled to interpret the long bill of fare, that the minimum charge for any semi-alcoholic beverage was £3. And he was beginning to suspect that the best value for such an exorbitant charge was probably two (separate) half-glasses of lager—when he heard her voice.

"Can I take your order?"

Over the top of his glasses he looked up at the young woman who stood in front of him. She was leaning forward, completely naked from the waist upwards, her long, pink skirt split widely to the top of her thigh.

"The lager, I think, please."

She made a note on the pad she held. "Would you like me to sit with you?"

"Yes, I would."

"You'd have to buy me a drink."

"All right."

She pointed to the very bottom of the card:

Flamenco Revenge—a marriage of green-eyed Chartreuse with aphrodisiac Cointreau.

Soho Wallbanger—a dramatic confrontation of voluptuous Vodka with a tantalizing taste of Tia Maria.

Eastern Ecstasy—an irresistible alchemy of rejuvenating Gin and pulse-quickening Campari.

Price: £6.00

£6.00!

"I'm sorry," said Browne-Smith, "but I just can't afford—"

"I can't sit with you if you won't buy me a drink."

"It's so terribly expensive, though, isn't it? I just can't aff—"

"All right!" The words were clipped and final, and she left his table, to return a few minutes later with his first small glass of lager, setting the meagre measure before him with studied indifference and departing immediately.

From the alcove behind him, Browne-Smith could hear the conversation distinctly:

"Where you from?"

"Ostrighlia."

"Nice there?"

"Sure is!"

"You'd like me to sit with you?"

"Sure would!"

"You'd have to buy me a drink."

"Just you nime it, bighby!"

Browne-Smith swallowed a mouthful of his flat and tepid lager and took stock of the situation. Apart from the proximate Australian, he could see only one other customer, a man of indeterminate age (forty? fifty? sixty?) who sat at the bar reading a book. In contrast to his balding pate and the grey-white patches at his temples, the neatly-trimmed and black-brown beard was quite devoid of grizzled hairs; and for a few seconds the fanciful notion occurred to Browne-Smith that the man might be in disguise, this notion being somewhat reinforced by the fact that he was wearing a pair of incongruous sun-glasses which masked the eyes whilst not, apparently, blurring the print of the page upon which he appeared so totally engrossed.

From where Browne-Smith sat, the décor looked universally cheap. The carpet, a continuation of the stairway crimson, was dirty and stained, with threadbare patches beneath most of the plastic tables; the chairs were flimsy, rickety, wickerwork structures which seemed barely capable of supporting the weight of any over-fleshed client; the walls and ceiling had clearly once been painted white, but were now grubby and stained with the incessant smoke of cigarettes. But there was one touch of culture—a most surprising one: the soberly-volumed background music was the slow movement of Mozart's "Elvira Madigan" piano concerto (played by Barenboim—Browne-Smith could have sworn it), and this seemed to him almost as incongruous as listening to Shakin' Stevens in St. Paul's Cathedral.

Another man was admitted through the curtain and was duly visited by the same white-breasted beauty who had brought his own lager; the man at the bar turned over another page of his book; the Australian, clearly audible still, was none too subtly prodding his hostess into revealing what exactly it was she was selling, because she'd got what he wanted and his only concern was the price she might be asking for it; the girl behind the bar had obviously exhausted whatever the *Daily Mirror* could prognosticate; and Barenboim had landed lightly upon the final notes of that ethereal movement.

Browne-Smith's glass was now empty, and the only two hostesses on view were happily supping whatever the management had decided were today's ingredients for Soho Wallbangers, Flamenco Revenges, *et al.* So he got up, walked over to the bar and sat himself down on a stool.

"I've got another one paid for, I think."

"I'll bring it to you."

"No, don't bother. I'll sit here."

"I said I'd bring it to you."

"You don't mind me sitting here, do you?"

"You si' down where you were—you understand English?" All pretence at civility had vanished, and her voice sounded hard and mean.

"All right," said Browne-Smith quietly. "I don't want to cause any trouble." He sat down at a table a few yards from the bar, and watched the girl, and waited.

"You still didn't 'ear wha' I *said,* did you?" The voice was now crudely menacing, but Browne-Smith decided that a few more rounds of small-arms fire could safely be expended; not *quite* time yet for the heavy artillery. He was enjoying himself.

"I *did* hear you, I assure you. But—"

"Look! I told you!" (Which she hadn't.) "If you want a bloody rub-off there's a sauna right across the road. OK?"

"But I don't—"

"I shan't tell you again, mister."

Browne-Smith stood up, and stepped slowly to the bar, where the man reading the book flicked over another page, disinterestedly neutral, it appeared, in the outcome of the escalating hostilities.

"I'd like a pint of decent beer, if you have one." He spoke quietly.

"If you don't want tha' lager—"

Abruptly Browne-Smith crashed his glass on the counter, and fixed the girl with his eyes. "Lager? Let me tell *you* something, miss! That's not lager—that's horse-piss!"

The battle odds had changed dramatically, and the girl had clearly lost her self-control as she pointed a shaking, carmined finger towards the crimson curtain: "Get out!"

"Oh no! I've paid for my drinks."

"You heard what the lady said." It was the man sitting reading his book by the bar. Although he had neither lifted his eyes one centimetre from the text, nor lifted, it seemed, his flat (West Country?) voice one semitone above its customary pitch, the brief words sounded ominously final.

But Browne-Smith, completely ignoring the man who had just spoken to him, continued to glare at the girl. "Never speak to me like that again!"

The hissed authority of these words reduced the girl to speechlessness, but the seated man had slowly closed his book, and now at last he raised his eyes. The fingers of his right hand crept across to the upper muscles of his left arm and, although as he eased himself off the bar-stool he stood some two or three inches shorter than Browne-Smith, he looked a dangerous adversary. He said nothing more.

The velvet curtains by which Browne-Smith had entered were only some three yards to his left, and there were several seconds during which a quick, if inglorious, exit could easily have been effected. But no such decision was taken; and before he could consider the situation further he felt his left wrist grasped powerfully, and found himself propelled towards a door marked "Private."

Two things he was to remember as his escort knocked quietly upon this door. First, he saw the look on the face of the man from Australia, a look that was three-parts puzzlement and one part panic; second, he observed the title of the book the bearded man was reading: *Know Your Köchel Numbers.*

The anonymous Australian, sitting no more than four or five yards from the door, was destined never to mention this episode to another living soul. And indeed, even had he reason to do so, it seems most improbable that he would have mentioned that enigmatic little moment, just before the door closed behind the two men, when the one of them who seemed to be causing the trouble, the one whose name he would never know, had suddenly looked at his wristwatch, and said in a voice that sounded inexplicably calm: "My goodness! I see it's exactly twelve noon."

For a few seconds after he had crossed the threshold of the office, Browne-Smith experienced that dazzling, zigzag pain again that seemed to saw its way across his brain, momentarily cutting him off from any recollection of himself and of what he was doing. But then it stopped—as suddenly as it had started—and he thought he was in control of things once more.

Looking out over the lawn of Second Quad, George Westerby had watched the tallish figure (several inches taller than himself) striding out towards the Porter's Lodge at 8:15 a.m. that same morning. Uppermost in his mind at that moment—and he gloried in it—was the realization that he would be seeing very little more of his detested colleague, Browne-Smith. He himself, George Westerby, having recently celebrated his sixty-eighth birthday, was retiring at last. Indeed, a removal firm had already been at work on his vast accumulation of books; and the treasured rows from more than half his shelves had been removed in blocks, stringed up, and stacked into the tea-chests that now occupied an uncomfortably large area of the floor space. And soon, of course, there would be the wooden crates, and the lumbering, muscled men who would transfer his precious possessions to the flat he had purchased in London. A smaller place, naturally, and one that might well pose a few storage problems. That could wait though, certainly until after his forthcoming holiday in the Aegean Isles . . . over to Asia across that azure sea. . . .

But even as he stood there by the window, nodding slowly and contentedly to himself for a few moments, it was Browne-Smith who still dominated his thoughts. It had always been "Browne-Smith" with him—not even "Malaria" Browne-Smith, as though such familiarity might compromise his eternal antagonism. There would be only a few more nights now when he would have to dine in Hall with that odious man; just a few more lunches, occasionally standing awkwardly proximate over the cold buffets; only one more College meeting, at the beginning of next week— the very last one. For the Trinity Term was almost over now; his last term, and very soon his last day and his last hours; and then the moment (when it came) of looking down for the very last time on that immaculate lawn. . . .

George Westerby was collectively conscious of all these things as he stood watching from his first-floor window on that chilly early morning of the 11th July. What he did not know at that time—what he could not have known—was that Lonsdale College was never again to welcome Browne-Smith within its quiet quads.

CHAPTER FOUR

Friday, 11th July

In which we have a tantalizing glimpse of high-class harlotry.

The taxi-driver knew the street, and Browne-Smith settled himself in the back seat with a heightened sense of excitement. He would have wished to savour these moments longer, but in less than five minutes the taxi pulled up at the kerb of Number 29, a large four-storied balconied building in a fashionable terrace just behind Russell Square. In general, although the original brickwork on the lower reaches of the walls had been smutted by traffic-fumes and smoke, the house seemed to have maintained its elegant façade with comparative ease. The black door, with its polished brass knobs and letter-box, was framed by white pillars; and the woodwork of the windows was also painted white, with neatly-kept window-boxes adding their splash of greens and reds. Black railings, set in concrete, were stretched along the front; behind which, after a gap of about five feet, the wall of the house continued down to a basement. On these railings a board had been affixed:

> Luxury Apartments for Sale or to Let
> Please apply: Brooks and Gilbert
> (Sole Agents) Tel. 01-483 2307
> Viewing by appointment only

Browne-Smith walked up the three shallow steps, and pressed the single bell, apprehensively fingering the blue card that was now in his inside jacket-pocket. He waited. But he had heard no sound of ringing on the other side of the great door, and he could see no sign of life. At this moment, and for the first time, the idea filtered into his mind that he might have been cruelly duped for the silly fool— the silly *old* fool—that he was, in going along with the whole disreputable and dishonourable business. He turned to look at the busy street and saw an aristocratic female disembarking from a taxi only a few doors away. No, it wasn't too late even now! He could just forget it all, hail the taxi. . . .

But the door had opened silently behind him.

"Can I help you?" (That West Country intonation again.)

"I'm a friend of Mr. Sullivan's." (Hardly the customary tone of his Mods tutorials—hesitant and slightly croaky.)

"You have an appointment?"

He took out the small, oblong card and handed it to her. The typewritten legend was exceedingly brief, but also (as Browne-Smith saw it) exceedingly significant: "Please admit bearer"—nothing else, except for that little constellation of asterisks clustered in the top right-hand corner.

The woman stood aside and beckoned him over the threshold, closing the door (again noiselessly) behind them. "You're an important client, sir, and we welcome you." She smiled appropriately as they moved through the large entrance-hall, carpeted in a light-olive shade, with the same carpeting leading up the wide staircase which faced the front door. She turned to him as she walked on ahead up these stairs, and Browne-Smith noticed her inappropriately ugly teeth as she smiled again. "All blue cards are on the first floor, sir. I'm afraid we haven't got our full complement of girls just for the moment—it's the evenings usually that we have our busiest time. But I'm sure you won't be disappointed in any way. No one's ever disappointed here."

On the first landing, she turned to him again, her eyes assessing him shrewdly, like a tailor mentally measuring some wealthy customer. Then, after looking along the corridor to left and right, she appeared to decide where the most appropriate prospects lay, for she opened the door im-

mediately across the landing with a brusqueness which
seemed clearly to betoken her mistress-ship of the establishment.

At a table immediately inside the room on the left sat a
woman of some forty summers, blonde and big-breasted,
wearing a low-cut, full-length purple gown; and, as the lady
of the house introduced her client, she stood up and slowly
smiled.

"You're free, I think, this afternoon, Yvonne?"

"Thees eevening, also, madame, eef you weesh it." The
blonde smiled bewitchingly again, showing her beautifully
even teeth. She was exquisitely made up, a moist lipstick
marking the contours of her sensuous mouth, her hair piled
immaculately on top of her finely-boned head.

"Is Paula free, too?"

"She weel be, madame. She 'ave a client for lernch,
but she weel be free aftair."

"Well—" (madame spoke directly to Browne-Smith)
"—if you're happy to stay here with Yvonne, sir?"

He swallowed and nodded his unequivocal assent.

"Good. I'll leave you, then. But you are to have everything you want, sir—I hope you understand that? Absolutely *everything*."

"I'm most grateful."

She turned to go. "You must know Mr. —er—Sullivan
very well, sir?"

"I was just able to do him a little favour, that's all. You
know how these things are."

"Of course. And you promise to let me know if there's
anything that Yvonne here can't—"

"I don't think you need worry."

Then madame was gone, and the back of Browne-
Smith's throat felt parched as he fought to stem the flood of
erotic imaginings that threatened to swamp him. He had
little help from the woman who, briefly resuming her seat
in order to make some entry in a red leather-bound diary on
the table, leant forward as she did so and revealed even to
the most casual glance that beneath her dress she was wearing little else—at least above her rather ample hips.

"I am weeth you now, sir." She rose from her chair and walked round to him. "Let me take your coat."

Browne-Smith took off the light-brown summer rain-coat he had worn continuously since leaving Oxford, and watched her as she folded it neatly over her left arm, slid her right hand under his elbow, and guided him over to a door at the far end of the room.

Compared with the somewhat austere and sparsely furnished room they had just left, this inner room was lavishly and (to Browne-Smith's tastes) rather luridly equipped. Two blood-red lamps, affixed to the inner wall, cast a subdued light around, and thick, yellow curtains, drawn fully across the single window, cut out all but the narrowest chink of natural light. The other furnishings were gaudily provocative with a cohort of multi-coloured cushions covering the long, low settee, and, behind that, bright yellow sheets and pillows on the widely welcoming bed, its coverlet already turned back. Opposite the settee was a tall, well-stocked, drinks-cabinet, its doors standing open; and beside it a film-projector, pointing a protruding snout towards the white expanse of wall to the left of the curtained casement. Pervading all was the heavy, heady smell of some sweet scent, and Browne-Smith felt a semi-permanent, priapic push between his loins.

"You'd like a dreenk?"

She went over to the cabinet and recited a comprehensive choice: whisky, gin, campari, vodka, rum, martini. . . .

"Whisky, please."

"Glenfeeddich?"

"My favourite."

"And mine."

There seemed to be two bottles of each drink, one of them as yet unopened, as though the liquid capacity of even the most dedicated toper had been nobly anticipated. And he watched her (why was he puzzled?) as she ripped the seal off a new bottle, poured out a half-tumbler of the pale malt-whisky, and brought it over to him.

"Aren't you going to have one, er—"

"Eevone. Please call me 'Eevone,' I call you 'sir'—because, madame, she inseest on eet. But for me—Eevone!"

Even as she spoke, Browne-Smith found himself thinking, albeit vaguely, that her French accent was carefully cultivated and—yes, completely phoney. But why worry about that? More important, for his own fastidious tastes, was the fear that someone else might enter the room. So he took a large gulp of Scotch and voiced his anxiety.

"We shan't be interrupted, shall we?"

"*Non, non!* Madame, you raymember, she say you 'ave everything you want? So? Eef you want me to lock the door, I lock eet. Eef you want Paula, per'aps, you 'ave Paula, OK? But I 'ope you want me, *non?*"

Phew!

She went over to the door and turned the key, went over to the cabinet and poured herself a gin-and dry-martini, and finally came to sit beside him on the settee, her thigh pressing closely against his own. She clinked their glasses: "I'm sure we 'ave a good time together, eh? I always like it eef I dreenk."

Browne-Smith took a further gulp of his Scotch, sensing even at this early stage that the alcohol was having an unwontedly powerful effect upon him.

"I feel you up a leetle?"

Momentarily he misunderstood her pronunciation of that second word; but when she took his glass he nodded in happy acquiescence, watching her in a wonderful anticipation as she walked away.

"You like my dress?" She was in front of him now, the replenished glass in her left hand. "Eet show off my figure, *non?*"

"You have a lovely figure."

"You theenk so? But eet ees so 'ot in 'ere. You take off your coat, per'aps?" She leaned over him, helping to remove his jacket, the dress soft against him, her body soft, the lighting soft; and he sat there passively as she slid her hands beneath the cuffs of his shirt, and deftly unfastened the cufflinks (Oxford University) before pushing the sleeves slowly up the arms. "Just to see eef you 'ave a leetle, what you call eet, 'tattoo'?"

"No, I haven't, actually."

"Nor 'ave I. But soon you weel be able to see for yourself, *non?*" She sat closely beside him again, and Browne-Smith gulped back another large mouthful of his drink and willed himself to relax for a while. But she gave him little chance, taking his right hand and placing it on the shoulder of her dress.

"You like that?" she asked.

My God! His hand fumbled for a few seconds with the material of the dress, and then slipped tentatively beneath it, feeling the soft flesh around her neck.

"Can I—?"

"You can do anytheeng." Even as she spoke those blissful words her eyes sparkled, and she jumped to her feet, pulling him up in turn with both hands. "But we 'ave a leetle feelm first, OK?"

Reluctantly, Browne-Smith did as he was bidden, taking his seat in an upright chair in front of the projector, and seeking to prepare himself for the voyeuristic aperitif. Clearly the pattern of events she'd suggested was not an unusual one; she, doubtless, must occasionally feel the need for some erotic stimulus. It was rather sad, this last fact, but he was too intelligent a man to feel surprised.

The scenes now witnessed on the white patch of wall beside the yellow curtaining were wilder by a dozen leagues than the few X-certificated films that Browne-Smith had paid to see at the ABC cinema during the Oxford vacations. It was a pity that the woman wasn't seated close to him; but (as she'd explained) unless she continually made some slight adjustments to the focussing mechanism, the technicolour delineation tended to drift out of true.

It was all so strangely *déjà vu*.

A man, in a smartly-cut business suit; a beautiful blonde in a full-length, purple gown; a few intimate drinks on a multi-cushioned settee; the man's hand slipping slowly inside the low-cut bodice and hoisting therefrom a bronzed, globed breast; then a teasingly slow, provocative undress on the part of the blonde, followed by much mutual grasping and gasping—before a finale that was fully orchestrated by climactic groans and an energetic spurting of semen.

The whirring, clicking projector was now switched off, and he felt her hands on his shoulders from behind.

"You like eet again?" She came round and sat on his knees. "Or would you rather 'ave *me*?"

He swallowed the first "*You!*" but managed the second.

"There ees a long zeep at the back of my dress—that's eet. Just pull down—pull! Yes, that's eet!"

Browne-Smith felt the sinuous movement of her hips pressing down on him as his fingers ventured across her naked back; and then she got up and walked over to the bed.

"Come and let me undress you."

Her back was turned away from him as she shrugged the dress off her shoulders, bent down to slip off her black, high-heeled shoes, stepped professionally out of her dress, and folded it neatly over the chair at the foot of the bed. Then she turned fully towards him, and he felt an enormously urgent need to take her immediately; but still she teetered on the brink of things, and he thought of the mercilessly tortured Tantalus and the illicit grapes that dangled just above his lips.

"One more leetle drink, per'aps?"

Browne-Smith, now almost in a delirium of anticipation, watched her as she walked over to the cabinet, watched her as she poured the two drinks, watched her as her beautifully-formed breasts bounced towards him once more.

"Just lie there a leetle meenite. You can 'ave me very soon."

She had disappeared through the only other door in the room, doubtless (judging by the flushing of water) a bathroom. And he, for his part, lay there almost fully clothed upon the yellow sheets, wondering in a hazily distanced sort of way just what was going on. Although his mouth seemed dry as the Sahara, he put down his drink untasted on the bedside-table, and for a while his mind grew clearer. Why had she used the *other* bottle of Glenfiddich? Perhaps . . . perhaps it had been watered down a bit?

Just as the Bursar always said at a Gaudy: "Let them have the good stuff first."

When, after what seemed an eternity, she returned, he watched her again, leaning half-upright on his right elbow. But his request was the oddest she had ever heard.

"Have you got any sort of *cream*, or something? My lips are awfully dry."

She fetched her handbag from the settee, opened the flap, and delved around for a few seconds. Then, unscrewing a circular container, she leaned over him, her breasts suspended only inches from his eyes, and smoothly smeared some cream along his lips.

"That ees better, *non?* Dreenk up, darleeng!"

She unfastened his tie; then unfastened the front of his shirt, one button at a time, at each stage her fingers splaying across his chest.

For Browne-Smith these moments were almost unbearably erotic, and he knew that he had little hope of lasting out much longer. Yet he made one further quite extraordinary request. "Can you open the curtains—just a little bit?"

When the woman returned she saw the man's jacket, hitherto folded at the foot of the bed, was now lying beside him; and as she looked down at his motionless body, she saw the tell-tale stain that seeped around the front of his well-cut, dark-blue trousers. His eyes were closed and his breathing steady, the right hand hanging loosely over the side of the bed, the index finger missing below the proximal inter-phalangeal joint. His glass, on the table beside his head, was now empty. She gently took his right arm and lay it alongside his body. Almost, for a moment or so, she felt a pang of tenderness. Then she hurriedly re-dressed, unlocked the door of the room, went out, and spoke in whispers to a man standing outside—a man who was reading a book entitled *Know Your Köchel Numbers*.

Her duties were done.

CHAPTER FIVE

Friday, 11th July

> *A woman of somewhat dubious morals seeks to relax, although such is her nature that she recalls too clearly, and too often, the duties she has been paid so handsomely to perform.*

In the latish evening of the day on which the events described in the previous chapter took place, a woman was seated alone in an upstairs flat, bedsitter-cum-bathroom-cum-kitchen, of a house situated in one of the many residential streets that lead south off the Richmond Road. Half an hour earlier she had walked from East Putney tube-station, and now she felt tired. Piccadilly to Earls Court, change trains, across the Thames to Putney—how many times had she made that tiresome journey? It would have been so much easier to live in Soho, and there had been no lack of opportunity on that score! But she enjoyed her two lives—her two spheres of existence which intersected at (almost) no single point. Here, in soberly bourgeois suburbia, she was a middle-aged woman with a job in the city. Here, she kept herself very much to herself, quietly, pleasantly, comfortably, dealing with rent and rates and household bills, and furnishing her few rooms at lavish expense. Yet these rooms were for *her* enjoyment only, since she had never invited another person into them, except for the cleaning woman (two hours per week). Except, too, for the man who had come to see her only four days ago.

The woman we are describing looked to be about forty, but was in fact some ten years older. Yet one could readily be forgiven for such misjudgement. She was a large-breasted woman, with hips that had put on several inches over recent years, but her legs were finely graceful still, her ankles slim and firm. There were, certainly, a few tell-tale lines at the corners of her mouth, and again at the sides of her eyes; but the mouth itself was as delicately, deliciously sensitive as it had always been, and the eyes were normally as clear and bright as a summer's noon in the Swedish hills.

Tonight, however, those self-same eyes were dull and sombre. Seated in an armchair, she crossed her nyloned legs, rested her blonde head upon her left arm, and stared down for many minutes at the richly-patterned Wilton carpet. She still felt that residual sense of triumph and achievement; but she felt, too, a certain tension and concern which, over the last few hours, had been growing inexorably into a sense of guilt-ridden remorse.

It had all had its beginnings early on the previous Monday morning, almost immediately after the Sauna Select (just off Brewer Street) had opened its doors to the men who frequented that establishment. There was nothing common, nothing mean about it all; just a gentlemanly and a ladylike understanding that with little fuss and large finance the whole gamut of erotic refinements was readily available. Many of the steady if unspectacular clients were men of middle or late-middle age; some of them were undisguisedly and indisputably ancient. But all were wealthy, since that was the *sine qua non* of the business. How else could the management afford the princessly salaries of its four assorted hostesses? For (as the woman so often reminded herself) it *was* a big salary—far better than her former wages as a popular stripper in the Soho clubs, commuting with her bulky case of costumes from one cramped dais to another.

It had been 10:35 a.m. when the man had come in. He'd wanted a sauna, he said; he wanted nothing else. That's what they all said; but soon the moisture and the heat and the inhibitions slowly dissipating in a world of steam and relaxation would almost always lead to something else. And this man? He had assessed the four of them with an almost embarrassing thoroughness—their figures, their complexions, their eyes—and he had chosen *her;* thereafter being escorted to the steam-room, and thence to one of the private massage parlours (£20 extra) in which the expertly-fingered and minimally-clad girls would exercise their skills.

He was sweating profusely under the belted white towelling that reached down to mid-thigh. She, for her part, cool and elegant, was dressed in the regulation white-cotton housecoat, with only the thinly transparent bra and pants beneath.

"Would you like to lie down on the couch, sir? On your back, please."

He had said nothing at that stage, obeying her suggestions mechanically and closing his eyes as she stood behind him, her fingers gently massaging the muscles round his neck.

"Nice?"

"Lovely!"

"Just relax!" She insinuated her hands beneath the towelling and massaged his shoulders with the tips of her strong and beautifully manicured fingers, working down from the neck towards the armpits—repeatedly, gently, sensually. And then, as she'd done a thousand times before, she walked round the couch and stood at his side, leaning over him, the top two buttons of her tunic already unfastened.

"Would you like me to undress while I massage you?" Wonderful question! And almost invariably an offer that couldn't be refused, even when the price of such an optional extra was clearly stated in advance.

It was a surprise to the woman, therefore, when her apparently pliable and co-operative client had slowly sat up, swung his legs off the couch, leaned forward to fasten the buttons of her tunic, pulled the white towelling back over his shoulders, and said "No."

But there followed an even bigger surprise.

"Look! I think I know you, and I certainly knew your father. Is it safe to talk here?"

Her father! Yes, she could still remember him. Those interminable rows she had heard so often from her lonely

bedroom when the amiable drunkard had finally reached
home from the local—rows apparently forgotten by the following dawns, when the household moved about its normal
business. Then, in 1939, he had been called up in the army,
when she had been only eight years old: and his death,
three years later, had seemed to her little more than the
indefinite prolongation of an already lengthy period of absence from her life. There had been many reminders of
him, of course: photographs, letters, clothes, shoes. But,
truth to tell, the death of her father had been an event that
was less-than-tragic and only dimly comprehended. But it
had been otherwise for her mother, who had wept so often
through those first few weeks and months. And it was
largely to try to compensate for such an uneven burden of
things that the young girl had tried so very hard with her
schoolwork, helped so regularly with the housework, and
even (later on) kept in check those symptoms of teenage
rebelliousness that had threatened to swamp all sense of
filial piety. As the years went by, she had gradually taken
over everything from an increasingly neurotic and feckless
mother, who had sunk into premature senility by her early
fifties, and into her grave before reaching her sixtieth year.

When the man had fastened up her buttons, she had
felt belittled and cheap—on the wrong side of the habitual
transaction. But she also felt deeply interested.

"Yes, it's safe," she said, finally answering his question.

"No microphones? No two-way mirrors?"

She shook her head. "About my father—"

"You don't remember me, do you?"

She looked at him: a man over sixty, perhaps; fairly
well-preserved by the look of him; head balding, teeth nic-
otined, jowls blue, chin somewhat sagging, but the mouth
still firm and not without some sensitivity. No, she couldn't
remember him.

"I called at your house once, but that was a long time
ago. You were, I don't know, fifteen or sixteen—still at
school, anyway, because your mother asked you to go and
do your homework in the kitchen. It was the year after the

war was over, and I'd known your father—we were in the same mob together. In fact, I was with him when he died."

"What do you want?" she asked abruptly.

"I want you to do something for me—something you'll be paid for doing—paid very well."

"What—?"

But he held up his hand. "Not now! You're living at 23A Colebourne Road—is that right?"

"Yes."

"I'd like to come and see you, if I may."

He had come the next evening, and talked whilst she listened. And, when she'd expressed her willingness to do what he asked, a deal was done, a partial payment made. And now, this very day, she had acted the role that he had asked of her, and the final payment had been made. A lot of easy money for a little easy work, and yet. . . .

Yes, it was that little "and yet" that caused her mind to fill with nagging doubts as she sat and sipped her China tea. She knew *enough*, of course—she'd insisted on that. But perhaps she should have insisted on knowing more, especially about the sequel to her own performance in the drama. They couldn't—they wouldn't, surely—have . . . *killed* him?

Her lips felt dry, and she reached for her handbag, opened the flap, and delved around for a few seconds before unscrewing a circular container—for the second time that day.

CHAPTER
SIX

Wednesday, 16th July

In which the Master of Lonsdale is somewhat indiscreet to a police inspector, and discusses his concern for one of his colleagues, and for the niceties of English grammar.

On the fifth morning after the events described in the preceding chapter, Detective Chief Inspector Morse, of the Thames Valley Constabulary, was seated in his office at Kidlington, Oxon. One half of him was semi-satisfied with the vagaries of his present existence; the other half was semi-depressed. Earlier that very morning he had sworn himself a solemn vow that the day ahead would be quite different. His recent consumption of food, tobacco, and alcohol had varied only within the higher degrees of addictive excess; and now, at the age of fifty-two, he had once again decided that a few days of virtually total abstinence was urgently demanded by stomach, lungs, and liver alike. He had arrived at his office, therefore, unbreakfasted, having already thrown away a half-full packet of cigarettes, and having left his half-empty wallet on the bedside-table. Get thou behind me, Satan! And, indeed, things had gone surprisingly well until about 11:30 a.m., when the Master of Lonsdale had rung through to HQ and invited Morse down to lunch with him.

"Half-past twelve—in my rooms—all right? We can have a couple of snifters first."

"I'd like that," Morse heard himself saying.

As he walked towards the Master's rooms in the first quad, Morse passed two young female students chattering to each other like a pair of monkeys.

"But surely *Rosemary's* expecting a first, isn't she? If she doesn't get one—"

"No. She told me that she'd made a *terrible* mess of the General Paper."

"So did I."

"And *me!*"

"She'll be awfully disappointed, though. . . ."

Yes, life was full of disappointments, Morse knew that better than most; and, as he half-turned, he watched the two young, lovely ladies as they walked out through the Porter's Lodge. They must be members of the college—two outward and happily visible signs of the fundamental change of heart that had resulted in the admission of women to these erstwhile wholly-masculine precincts. Now when he himself had been up at St. John's. . . But, abruptly, he switched off the memories of those dark, disastrous days.

"What'll it be, Morse? No beer, I'm afraid but—gin and tonic—gin and French?"

"Gin and French—lovely!" Morse reached over and took a cigarette from the well-stocked open box on the table.

The Master beamed in avuncular fashion as he poured his mixtures with a practised hand. He had changed little in the ten years or so that Morse had known him: going to fat a little, but as distinguished-looking a man now, in his late fifties, as he had been in his late forties; a tall man, with that luxuriant grey hair still framing the large head; the suits (famed throughout the University) as flamboyant as ever they were, and today eye-catchingly complemented by a waistcoat of green velvet. A successful man, and a proud man. A Head of a House.

"You've got women here now, I see," said Morse.

"Yes, old boy. We were almost the last to give in—but, well, it's been a good thing on the whole. Very good, some of them."

"Good-looking, you mean?"

The Master smiled. "A few."

"They sleep in?"

"Some of them. Still, some of them always did, didn't they?"

"I suppose so," said Morse; and his mind drifted back to those distant days just after the war, when he had come up to Oxford with an exhibition in Classics from one of the Midland grammar schools.

"Couple of firsts this year—among the girls, I mean. One in Greats, one in Geography. Not bad, eh? In fact the Classics girl, Jane—" Suddenly the Master stopped and leaned forward earnestly, awkwardly twiddling the large, onyx dress-ring on the little finger of his left hand. "Look, Morse! I shouldn't have said—what I just said. The class-lists won't be out for another week or ten days—"

Morse waved his right hand across the space between them, as though any mental recollection of the indiscretion had already been expunged. "I didn't hear a word you said, Master. I know what you were going to tell me, though."

"Oh?"

"She's got the top first in the University, and she'll soon get a summons for a congratulatory viva. Right?"

The Master nodded. "Super girl—bit of a honey, too, Morse. You'd have liked her."

"Still would, I shouldn't wonder."

The Master's eyes were twinkling with merriment now. How he enjoyed Morse's company!

"She'll probably marry some lecherous sod," continued Morse, "and end up with half a dozen whining infants."

"You're not exactly full of the joys of summer."

"Just envious. Still there are more important things in life than getting a first in Greats."

"Such as?"

Morse considered the question a few moments before shaking his head. "I dunno."

"I'll tell you one thing. There's not likely to be anything much more important for *her*. We shall probably offer her a junior fellowship here."

"You mean you've already offered her one."

"Please don't forget, will you, that I—er—I shouldn't have said anything about all this. I'm normally very discreet."

"Must be the drink," said Morse, looking down into his empty glass.

"Same again? Mixture about right?"

"Fraction more gin, perhaps?" Morse reached for another cigarette as the Master refilled the glasses. "I suppose she could take her pick of all the undergrads?"

"*And* the dons!"

"You never married, did you, Master."

"Nor did you."

For some minutes the two of them sat silently sipping. Then Morse asked: "Has she got a mother?"

"Jane Summers, you mean?"

"You didn't mention her surname before."

"Odd question! I don't know. I expect so. She's only, what, twenty-two, twenty-three. Why do you ask?"

But Morse was hardly listening. In the quad outside it had been comparatively easy to pull the curtain across the painful memories. But now? Not so! His eyes seemed on the point of shedding a gin-soaked tear as he thought again of his own sad days at Oxford. . . .

"You listening?"

"Pardon?" said Morse.

"You don't seem to be paying much attention to what I'm saying."

"Sorry! Must be the booze." His glass was empty again and the Master needed no prompting.

"Will you keep a gentle eye on things for me, then? You see, I'm probably off myself this weekend for a few days."

"Few weeks, do you mean?"

"I'm not sure yet. But if you could just, as I say, keep an eye on things—you'd put my mind at rest."

"Keep an eye on *what*?"

"Well, it's just—so *unlike* Browne-Smith, that's all. He's the most pedantic and pernickity fellow in the University. It's—it's odd. No arrangements, none. Just this note left at the lodge. No apology for absence from the college meeting; nothing to the couple of students he'd arranged to see."

"You've got the note?"

The Master took a folded sheet from his dove-grey jacket and handed it over:

> Please keep any mail for me here. I shall be away for several days. Sudden irresistable offer—quite out of the blue. Tell my scout to look after my effects, i.e. to keep the rooms well dusted, put the laundry through and cancel all meals until further notice.
>
> B-S

Morse felt a tingle in his veins as he read through the brief, typewritten message. But he said nothing.

"You see," said the Master, "I just don't think he wrote that."

"No?"

"No, I don't."

"When did the Lodge get this?"

"Monday morning—two days ago."

"And when was he last seen here?"

"Last Friday. In the morning, it was. He left college at about quarter-past eight, to catch the London train. One of the fellows here saw him on the station."

"Did this note come through the post?"

"No. The porter says it was just left there."

"Why are you so sure he didn't write it?"

"He just *couldn't* have written it. Look, Morse, I've known him for twenty-odd years, and there was never a man, apart from Housman, who was so contemptuous about any solecism in English usage. He was almost paranoiac about things like that. You see, he always used to draft the minutes of the college meetings, and even a comma out of place in the final version would bring down the wrath of the gods on the college secretary. He even used to type a draft before he'd put a bloody notice on the board!"

Morse looked at the letter again. "You mean he'd have put commas after 'sudden'—and 'through'?"

"By Jove, yes! He'd *always* use commas there. But there's something else. Browne-Smith was the *only* man in England, I should think, who invariably argued for a comma after 'i.e.'"

"Mm."

"You don't sound very impressed."

"Ah! But I am. I think you may be right."

"Really?"

"You think he's got a bird somewhere?"

"He's never had a 'bird,' as you put it."

"Is Jane Summers still in residence?"

The Master laughed aloud with genuine amusement. "I saw her this morning, Morse, if you must know."

"Did you tell her she'd got a first?" A smile was playing slowly around Morse's mouth, and the Master's shrewd eyes were again upon him.

"Not much point pretending with you, is there? But no! No, I *didn't* tell her that. But I did tell her that perhaps she had every reason to be—er, let's say, optimistic about her—ah, future. Anyway, it's time we went down for lunch. You ready to eat?"

"Can I keep this?" Morse held up the single sheet, and the Master nodded.

"Seriously, I'm just a fraction worried. And you just said, didn't you, that I might be right?"

"You *are* right. At least, you're almost certainly right in suggesting that he didn't *type* it. He could have dictated it, of course."

"Why are you so sure?"

"Well," said Morse, as the Master locked the door behind them, "he was a literary pedant for a good many years before *you* met him. He was one of my 'Mods' tutors, you see; and even then he'd bark away at the most trivial sort of spelling mistake as if it were the sin against the Holy Ghost. At the time, of course, it didn't seem to matter two farts in the universe; but in an odd sort of way I came to respect his views—and I still do. I'd never let a spelling mistake go through *my* secretary—not if I could help it."

"Never?"

"*Never!*" said Morse, his grey-blue eyes sober and se-rious as the two men lingered on the landing outside the Master's rooms. "And you can be absolutely sure of one thing, Master. Browne-Smith would have died sooner than misspell 'irresistible.'"

"You don't think—you don't think he *is* dead?"

"'Course he's not!" said Morse, as the two old friends walked down the stairs.

CHAPTER SEVEN

Week beginning Wednesday, 16th July

In which those readers impatiently waiting to encounter the first corpse will not be disappointed, and in which interesting light is thrown on the character of the detective, Morse.

It had been 2:30 p.m. when Morse finally left Lonsdale; and after stocking himself up from a tobacconist's shop just along The High, he was back in his Kidlington office just before three o'clock, where nothing much appeared to have happened during his absence.

On leaving Lonsdale, he had promised the Master to "keep an eye on things" (a quite meaningless phrase, as Morse saw it) should any aspect of Browne-Smith's sudden departure take on a slightly more sinister connotation.

To an observer, Morse's eyes would have appeared slightly "set," as Shakespeare has it, and his mood was mellowly maudlin. And as he sat there, his freely-winged imagination glided easily back to the fateful days of his time at Oxford . . .

After eighteen months as a National Serviceman in the Royal Signals Regiment, Morse had come up to St. John's College, where his first two years were the happiest and most purposeful of his life. He had worked hard at his texts, attended lectures regularly, been prompt with unseens and compositions; and it had been no surprise to his tutors when such an informed and intelligent young man had duly gained a first in Classical Moderations. With two years ahead of him—two years in which to study for Greats—the future seemed to loom as sure as the sun-bright day that would follow the rosy-fingered dawn—particularly so, since the slant of Morse's mind was ideally suited to the work ahead of him in History, Logic, and Philosophy. But in the middle of his third year he had met the girl who matched the joy of all his wildest dreams.

She was already a graduate of Leicester University, whence a series of glowing testimonials had proved sufficiently impressive for her application to take a D.Phil. at Oxford to be accepted by St. Hilda's. For her first term, she had been allotted digs way out in the distances of Cowley Road. But amidst the horsehair sofas and the sombre, dark-brown furnishings, she had been unhappy and had jumped at the opportunity of a smaller flat in Number 22 St. John Street (just off St. Giles's) at the start of the Hilary Term. It was so much brighter, so much nearer the heart of things, and only a short walk from the Bodleian Library, where she spent so much of her time. She felt happy in her new room. Life was good.

At this same time it was customary for the Dean of St. John's to farm out most of his third-year undergraduates to some of the nearby College property and, from the start of the Michaelmas term, Morse had moved into St. John's Road: Number 24.

They first met one night in late February, during the interval of the OUDS's production of *Doctor Faustus* at the New Theatre, only some fifty yards or so away, in Beaumont Street. Morse had finally managed to order a pint of beer at the crowded bar when he felt a lightly-laid hand upon his shoulder—and turned round to find a pale face, the blonde hair high upswept, the hazel eyes looking into his with an air of pleading diffidence.

"Have you just ordered?"

"Yes—I'll soon be out of your way."

"You wouldn't mind, would you, ordering a drink for me as well?"

"Pleasure!"

"Two gins-and-tonics, please." She pushed a pound-note into his hand—and was gone.

She was seated in a far corner of the bar, next to a dark-haired dowdy-looking young woman; and Morse, after negotiating his way slowly through the throng, carefully placed the drinks on the table.

"You didn't mind, did you?"

It was the blonde who had spoken, looking up at him with widely innocent eyes; and Morse found himself looking at her keenly—noting her small and thinly-nostrilled nose, noting the tiny dimples in her cheeks, and the lips that parted (almost mischievously now) over the rather large but geometrically regular teeth.

"'Course not! It's a bit of a squash in here, isn't it?"

"You enjoying the play?"

"Yes. Are you?"

"Oh yes! I'm a great Marlowe fan. So's Sheila, here. Er—I'm sorry. Perhaps you don't know each other?"

"I don't know *you*, either!" said Morse.

"There you are! What did I tell you?" It was the dark girl who had taken up the conversation. She smiled at Morse: "Wendy here said she recognized *you*. She says you live next door to her."

"Really?" Morse stood there, gaping ineffectually.

A bell sounded in the bar, signalling the start of the last act; and Morse, calling upon all his courage, asked the two girls if they might perhaps like to have a drink with him after the performance.

"Why not?" It was the saturnine Sheila who had answered. "We'd love to, Wendy, wouldn't we!"

It was agreed that the trio should meet up again in the cocktail-bar of the Randolph, a stone's-throw away, just along the street.

For Morse, the last act seemed to drag its slow length interminably along, and he left the theatre well before the end. The name "Wendy" was re-echoing through his mind as once the woods had welcomed "Amaryllis." With the bar virtually deserted, he sat and waited expectantly. Ten minutes. Fifteen minutes. The bar was filling up now, and twice, with some embarrassment, Morse had assured other customers that, yes, there *was* someone sitting in each of the empty seats at his table.

She came at last—Sheila, that is—looking around for him, coming across, and accepting his offer of a drink.

"What will—er—Wendy have?"

"She won't be coming, I'm afraid. She says she's sorry but she suddenly remembered—"

But Morse was no longer listening for now the night seemed drear and desolate. He bought the girl a second drink; then a third. She left at ten-thirty to catch her bus, and Morse watched with relief as she waved half-heartedly to him from the bar entrance.

It was trying to snow as Morse walked slowly back to St. John Street, but he stopped where he knew he would stop. On the right of the door of Number 22, he saw four names, typed and slotted into folders, a plastic bell-push beside each one of them. The first name was "Miss W. Spencer (Top Floor)," but no light shone at the highest window, and Morse was soon climbing the stairs to his cold bed-sitter.

For the next three days he spent much of the time hanging about in the vicinity of St. John Street, missing lectures, missing meals, and missing, too, any sight of the woman he was aching to see once more. Had she been called away? Was she ill? The whole gamut of tragic forebodings presented itself to his mind as he frittered away his hours and his energies in fruitless and futile imaginings. On the fourth evening he walked over to the Randolph, drank two double-Scotches, walked back to St. John Street, and with a thumping heart rang the bell at the top of the panel. And, when the door opened, she was standing there, a smile of gentle recognition in her eyes.

"You've been a long time," she said.

"I didn't quite know—"

"You knew where to find me—I told you that."

"I—"

"It wasn't *you* who made the first move, was it?"

"I—"

"Would you like to come in?"

Impetuously—even that first night—Morse told her that he loved her; and she, for her part, told him how very glad she was that they had met. After that, their days and weeks and months were spent in long, idyllic happiness: they walked together across the Oxfordshire countryside; went to theatres, cinemas, concerts, museums; spent much time in pubs and restaurants; and, after a while, much time in bed together, too. But, during those halcyon days, both were neglecting the academic work that was expected of them. At the end of the Trinity term, Morse was gently reminded by his tutor that he might be in danger of failing to satisfy the examiners the following year unless he decided to mount a forceful assault upon the works of Plato during the coming vacation. After a similar interview with her own supervisor, Wendy Spencer was firmly informed that unless her thesis began to show more obvious signs of progress, her grant—and therewith her doctorate—would be in serious jeopardy.

Surprisingly, perhaps, it was Morse who saw the more clearly the importance of some academic success—and who sought the more anxiously to promote it. But such success was not to be. Just before the Christmas vac a tearful Wendy announced that her doctorate was terminated; her grant, w.e.f. January 1st, withheld. Yet the two of them lived on very much as before: Wendy stayed on in her digs, and almost immediately got a job as a waitress in the Randolph; Morse tried hard to curb his beer consumption and occasionally read the odd chapter of Plato's *Republic*.

Ironically, it was one day before the anniversary of their first, wonderful evening together that Wendy received the telegram, informing her that her widowed mother had suffered a stroke, and that help was urgently required. So she had gone home—and stayed there. Scores of letters passed between the lovers during the dark months that followed; and twice Morse had made the journey to the West Country to see her. But he was very short of money now; and slowly he was learning to assimilate the truth that (for some reason) her mother was a more important figure in Wendy's life than he was. His performances for his tutors were now so pathetically poor that his college exhibition was rescinded, and he had the humiliating task of writing to beg his county authority to make up the deficit. Then, three weeks before Greats, he had received his last letter from her: she could not see him again; she had almost ruined his life already; she had a duty to stay with her mother, and had irrevocably decided to do so; she had loved him—she had loved him desperately—but now they had come to the end; she implored him not to reply to her letter; she urged him to do himself some semblance of justice in his imminent examination; *that* would always be important for her. Morse had immediately sent a telegram, begging her to meet him once more. But he received no reply—and had no money for a further journey. In his despair, he did nothing—absolutely nothing.

Two months later he learned that he had failed Greats; and, although the news was no surprise, he departed from Oxford a withdrawn and silent young man, bitterly belittled, yet not completely broken in spirit. It had been his sadly disappointed old father, a month or so before his death, who suggested that his only son might find a niche somewhere in the police force.

Morse's attractive young secretary came into the office and handed over his letters for signature.

"Do you want to dictate the others, sir?"

"A little later. I'll give you a ring."

After she had gone, he continued his earlier train of thought—but not for long. In any case, there was nothing more to recall. Of Wendy Spencer he had never heard another word. She would still be alive, though, surely? Even at that minute—that very second—she'd be *somewhere*. He repeated to himself the line from "Wessex Heights": "But time cures hearts of tenderness—and now I can let her go." It was a lie, of course. But so it had been for Hardy.

Nor had Morse ever met any of his Greats examiners since he had first come down from Oxford. Yet even now he could remember with dramatic clarity the six names that were subscribed to the class-list on that bleak day some thirty years ago:

Wells (Chairman)
Styler
Stockton
Sherwin-White
Austin
Browne-Smith

During the following week Morse did nothing about his tenuous promise to the Master. Well, virtually nothing. He *had* rung Lonsdale early on the Monday morning, but neither the Master, nor the Vice-Master, nor the Senior Fellow, nor the Bursar, was on the premises. Everyone had either gone or was about-to-be gone. With the heavy work over for another academic year, the corporate body of the University appeared to be taking a collective siesta. The thought suddenly occurred to Morse that this would be a marvellous time to murder a few of the doddery old bachelor dons. No wives to worry about their whereabouts; no families to ring their fathers from railway-stations; no landladies to whine about the unpaid rents. In fact, nobody would miss most of them *at all*—not, that is, until the middle of October.

It was on Wednesday, 23rd July, two days after his abortive phone-call to Lonsdale, that Morse himself, in mid-afternoon, received the news, recognizing Sergeant Lewis's voice immediately.

"We've got a body, sir—or at least part—"

"Where are you?"

"Thrupp, sir. You know the—"

"'Course I know it!"

"I think you'd better come."

"I've got a lot of correspondence to get on with—*you* can handle things, can't you?"

"We fished it out of the canal."

"Lots of people chuck 'emselves into—"

"I don't think this one drowned himself, sir," said Lewis quietly.

So Morse got the Lancia out of the yard, and drove the few miles out to Thrupp.

CHAPTER
EIGHT

Wednesday, 23rd July

*The necrophobic Morse reluctantly surveys a
corpse, and converses with a cynical and ageing
police-surgeon.*

Two miles north of police headquarters in Kidlington,
on the main A423 road to Banbury, an elbow turn to the
right leads, after only three hundred yards or so, to the Boat
Inn, which, together with about twenty cottages, a farm,
and a depot of the Inland Waterways Executive, comprises
the tiny hamlet of Thrupp. The inn itself, only some thirty
yards from the waters of the Oxford Canal, has served gen-
erations of boatmen, past and present. But the working
barges of earlier times, which brought down coal from the
Midlands and shipped up beer from the Oxford breweries,
have now yielded place to the privately-owned long-boats
and pleasure-cruisers which ply their way placidly along the
present waterway.

Chief Inspector Morse turned right at the inn, then
left along the narrow road stretching between the canal and
a row of small, grey-stoned, terraced cottages, their doors
and multi-paned windows painted a clean and universal
white. At almost any other time, Thrupp would have
seemed a snugly secluded little spot; but already Morse
could see the two white police cars pulled over on to the
tow-path, beside a sturdy-looking drawbridge; and an ambulance, its blue light flashing, parked a little further
ahead, where the road petered out into a track of grass-

grown gravel. It is strange to relate (for a man in his profession) that in addition to incurable acrophobia, arachnophobia, myophobia, and ornithophobia, Morse also suffered from necrophobia; and had he known what awaited him now, it is doubtful whether he would have dared to view the horridly disfigured corpse at all.

A knot of thirty or so people, most of them from the gaudily-painted houseboats moored along the waterway, stood at a respectful distance from the centre of activities; and Morse, pushing his way somewhat officiously through, came face to face immediately with a grim-looking Lewis.

"Nasty business, sir!"

"Know who it is?"

"Not much chance."

"What? You can *always* tell who they are—doesn't matter how long they've been in the water. You know that, surely? Teeth, hair, finger-nails, toe-nails—"

"You'd better come and look at him, sir."

"Ha! Know it's a 'him' do we? Well, that's something. Reduces the population by about 50 per cent at a stroke, that does."

"You'd better come and look at him," repeated Lewis quietly.

A uniformed police constable and two ambulance men moved aside as Morse walked towards the green tarpaulin sheet that covered a body recently fished from the murky-looking water. For a few moments, however, he was more than reluctant to pull back the tarpaulin. Instead, his dark eyebrows contracted to a frown as mentally he traced the odd configuration of the bulge beneath the winding-sheet. Surely the body had to be that of a child, for it appeared to be about three and a half feet long—no more; and Morse's up-curved nostrils betokened an even grislier revulsion. Adult suicide was bad enough. But the death of a child— agh! Accident? *Murder*?

Morse told the four men standing there to shield him from the silent onlookers as he pulled back the tarpaulin and—after only a few seconds—replaced it. His cheeks had grown ashen pale, and his eyes seemed stunned with hor-

ror. He managed only two hoarsely-spoken words: "My
God!"

He was still standing there, speechless and shaken,
when a big, battered old Ford braked sharply beside the
ambulance, from it emerging a mournful, hump-backed
man who looked as though he should have taken late retire-
ment ten years earlier. He greeted Morse with a voice that
matched his lean, lugubrious mien.

"I thought I'd find you in the bar, Morse."

"They're closed."

"You don't sound very cheerful, old man."

Morse pointed vaguely behind him, towards the sheet,
and the police surgeon immediately knelt to his calling.

"Phew! *Very* interesting!"

Morse, his back still turned on the corpse, heard himself mutter something that vaguely concurred with such a
finding, and thereafter left his sanguine colleague utterly in
peace.

Slowly and carefully the surgeon examined the body,
methodically entering notes into a black pocket-book.
Much of what he wrote would be unintelligible to one un-
versed in forensic medicine. Yet the first few lines were
phrased with frightening simplicity:

> First appearances: male (60-65?); Caucasian; torso
> well nourished (bit too well?); head (missing) sev-
> ered from shoulders (amateurishly?) at roughly
> the fourth cervical vertebra; hands l. & r. missing,
> the wrists cut across the medial ligaments; legs
> l. & r. also missing, severed from torso about 5-6
> inches below hip-joint (more professionally done?)
> skin—"washerwoman effect.". . .

Finally, and with some difficulty, the surgeon rose to
his feet and stood beside Morse, holding his lumbar regions
with both hands as though in chronic agony.

"Know a cure for lumbago, Morse?"

"I thought *you* were the doctor."

"Me? I'm just a poorly-paid pathologist."

"You get lumbago in mid-*summer*?"

"Mid-*every*-bloody-season!"

"They say a drop of Scotch is good for most things."

"I thought you said they're closed."

"Emergency, isn't it?" Morse was beginning to feel slightly better.

One of the ambulance men came up to him. "All right to take it away?"

"Might as well."

"No!" It was the surgeon who spoke. "Not for the moment. I want to have a few words with the chief inspector here first."

The ambulance man moved away and the surgeon sounded unwontedly sombre. "You've got a nasty case on your hands here, Morse, and—well, I reckon you ought to have a look at one or two things while we're *in situ*, as it were—you *were* a classicist once, I believe? Any clues going'll pretty certainly be gone by the time I start carving him up."

"I don't think there's much point in that, Max. You just give him a good going-over—that'll be fine!"

In kindly fashion, Max put a hand on his old friend's shoulder. "I know! Pretty dreadful sight, isn't it? But I've missed things in the past—you know that! And if—"

"All right. But I need a drink first, Max."

"*After.* Don't worry—I know the landlord."

"So do I," said Morse.

"OK, then?"

"OK!"

But, as the surgeon drew back the tarpaulin once more, Morse found himself quite incapable of looking a second time at that crudely jagged neck. Instead he concentrated his narrowed eyes upon the only limbs that someone—*someone* (already the old instincts were quickened again)—had felt it safe to leave intact. The upper part of the man's body was dressed in a formal, dark-blue, pinstriped jacket, matching the material of the truncated trousers below; and, beneath the jacket, in a white shirt, adorned with a plain rust-red tie—rather awkwardly fastened. Morse shuddered as the surgeon peeled off the sodden jacket, and placed the squelching material by the side of the dismembered torso.

"You want the trousers too?—what's left of 'em?"

Morse shook his head. "Anything in the pockets?"

The surgeon inserted his hands roughly into the left and right pockets; but his fingers showed through the bottom of each, and Morse felt as sick as some sensitively-palated patient in the dentist's chair having a wax impression taken of his upper jaw.

"Back pocket?" he suggested weakly.

"Ah!" The surgeon withdrew a sodden sheet of paper, folded over several times, and handed it to Morse. "See what I mean? Good job we—"

"You'd have found it, anyway."

"Think so? Who's the criminologist here, Morse? They pay *me* to look at the bodies—not a lump of pulp like that. I'd have sent the trousers to Oxfam, like as not—better still, the Boy Scouts, eh?"

Morse managed to raise a feeble grin, but he wanted the job over.

"Nothing else?"

Max shook his head; and as Morse (there being nothing less nauseating to contemplate) looked vaguely down along the outstretched arms, the surgeon interrupted his thoughts.

"Not much good, arms, you know. Now if you've got teeth—which in our case we have not got—or—"

But Morse was no longer listening to his colleague's idle commentary. "Will you pull his shirt-sleeves up for me, Max?"

"Might take a bit of skin with 'em. Depends how long—"

"Shut up!"

The surgeon carefully unfastened the cuff-links and pushed the sleeves slowly up the slender arms. "Not exactly a weightlifter, was he?"

"No."

The surgeon looked at Morse curiously. "You expecting to find a tattoo or something, with the fellow's name stuck next to his sweetheart's?"

"You never know your luck, Max. There might even be a name-tape on his suit somewhere."

"Somehow I don't reckon you're going to have too much luck in this case," said the surgeon.

"Perhaps not. . . ." But Morse was hardly listening. He felt the sickness rising to the top of his gullet, but not before he'd noticed the slight contusion on the inner hollow between the left biceps and the fore-arm. Then he suddenly turned away from the body and retched up violently on the grass.

Sergeant Lewis looked on with a sad and vulnerable concern. Morse was his hero, and always would be. But even heroes had their momentary weaknesses, as Lewis had so often learned.

CHAPTER
NINE

Wednesday, 23rd July

*In which Morse's mind drifts elsewhere as the po-
lice-surgeon enunicates some of the scientific prin-
ciples concerning immersion in fluids.*

It was later that same afternoon that Morse, Lewis,
and the police surgeon presented themselves at the Boat
Inn, where the landlord, sensibly circumspect, informed
the trio that it would of course be wholly improper for him
to serve any alcoholic beverages at the bar; on the other
hand the provision of three chairs in a back room and a
bottle of personally-purchased Glenfiddich might not perhaps be deemed to contravene the nation's liquor laws.

"How long's he been dead?" was Morse's flatly-spoken,
predictable gambit, and the surgeon poured himself a liberal tumbler before deigning to reply.

"Good question! I'll have a guess at it tomorrow."

Morse poured himself an equally liberal portion, his
sour expression reflecting a chronic distrust in the surgeon's
calling.

"A week, perhaps?"

The surgeon merely shrugged his shoulders.

"Could be longer, you mean?"

"Or shorter."

"Oh Christ! Come off it, Max!" Morse banged the bottle down on the table, and Lewis wondered if he himself
might be offered a dram. He would have refused, of course,
but the gesture would have been gratifying.

The surgeon savoured a few sips with the slow dedication of a man testing a dubious tooth with a mouthwash, before turning to Morse, his ugly face beatified: "Nectar, old man!"

Morse, likewise, appeared temporarily more interested in the whisky than in any problems a headless, handless, legless corpse might pose to the Kidlington CID. "They tell me the secret's in the water of those Scottish burns."

"Nonsense! It's because they manage to get *rid* of the water."

"Could be!" Morse nodded more happily now. "But while we're talking of water, I just asked you—"

"You know nothing about water, Morse. Listen! If you find a body immersed in fresh water, you've got the helluva job finding out what happened. In fact, one of the trickiest problems in forensic medicine—about which you know bugger-all, of course—is to prove whether death *was* due to drowning."

"But this fellow wasn't drowned. He had his head—"

"Shut up, Morse. You asked how long he'd been in the canal, right? You didn't ask me who sawed his head off!"

Morse nodded agreement.

"Well, *listen*, then! There are five questions I'm paid to ask myself when a body's found immersed in water, and in this particular case you wouldn't need a genius like me to answer most of them. First, was the person alive when entering the water? Answer: pretty certainly, no. Second, was death due to immersion? Answer: equally certainly, no. Third, was death rapid? Answer: the question doesn't apply, because death took place elsewhere. Fourth, did any other factors contribute to death? Answer: almost certainly, yes; the poor fellow was likely to have been clinically dead when somebody chopped him up and chucked him in the canal. Fifth, where did the body enter the water? Answer: God knows! Probably where it was found—as most of them are. But it could have drifted a fair way, in certain conditions. With a combination of bodily gases and other internal reactions, you'll often find a corpse floating up to the surface and then—"

But Morse interrupted him, turning to Lewis: "How *did* we find him?"

"We had a call from a chap who was fishing there, sir. Said he'd seen something looking like a body half-floating under the water, just where we found him."

"Did you get his name—this fisherman's?" Morse's question was sharp, and to Lewis his eyes seemed to glint with a frightening authority.

"I wasn't there myself, sir. I got the message from Constable Dickson."

"He took down the name and address, of course?"

"Not quite, sir," gulped Lewis. "He got the name all right, but—"

"—the fellow rang off before giving his address!"

"You can't really blame—"

"Who's blaming *anybody*, Lewis? What *was* his name, by the way?"

"Rowbotham. Simon Rowbotham."

"Christ! That's an unlikely sounding name."

"But Dickson got it down all right, sir. He asked the fellow to spell it for him—he told me that."

"I see I shall have to congratulate Constable Dickson the next time I have the misfortune to meet him."

"We're only talking about a name, sir." Lewis was feeling that incipient surge of frustrated anger he'd so often experienced with Morse.

"*Only?* What are you talking about? '*Simon?*' With a surname like '*Rowbotham*'? Lew-is! Now *George* Rowbotham—that's fine, that squares with your actual proletarian parentage. Or Simon *Carruthers*, or something—that's what you'd expect from some aristocrat from Saffron Walden. But *Simon Rowbotham*? Come off it, Lewis. The fellow who rang was making it up as he went along."

The surgeon, who had remained sipping placidly during this oddly intemperate exchange, now decided it was time to rescue the hapless Lewis. "You do talk a load of nonsense, Morse. I've never known your first name, and I don't give a sod what it is. For all I know, it's 'Eric' or 'Ernie' or something. But so bloody *what*?"

Morse, who had ever sought to surround his Christian name in the decent mists of anonymity, made no reply. Instead, he poured himself another measure of the pale yellow spirit, thereafter lapsing into silent thought.

It was Max who picked up the thread of the earlier discussion. "At least you're not likely to get bogged down in any doubts about accident or suicide—unless you find some boat-propeller's sliced his head off—and his hands—and his legs."

"No chance of that?"

"I haven't examined the body yet, have I?"

Morse grunted with frustration. "I asked you, and I ask you again. How long's he been in the water?"

"I just told you. I haven't—"

"Can't you try a feeble bloody guess?"

"Not all that long—in the water, that is. But he may have been dead a few days before then."

"Have a guess, for Christ's sake!"

"That's tricky."

"It's always 'tricky' for you, isn't it? You do actually think the fellow's *dead*, I suppose?"

The surgeon finished his whisky, and poured himself more, his lined face creasing into something approaching geniality. "Time of death? That's always going to play a prominent part in your business, Morse. But it's never been my view that an experienced pathologist—such as myself—can ever really put too much faith in the accuracy of his observations. So many variables, you see—"

"Forget it!"

"Ah! But if someone actually *saw* this fellow being chucked in—well, we'd have a much better idea of things, um?"

Morse nodded slowly and turned his eyes to Lewis; and Lewis, in turn, nodded his own understanding.

"It shouldn't take long, sir. There's only a dozen or so houses along the towpath."

He prepared to go. Before leaving, however, he asked one question of the surgeon. "Have you got the slightest idea, sir, when the body might have been put in the canal?"

"Two, three days ago, sergeant."

"How the hell do you know that?" growled Morse after Lewis had gone.

"I *don't* really. But he's a polite fellow, your Lewis, isn't he? Deserves a bit of help, as I see it."

"About two or three days, then. . . ."

"Not much more—and probably been dead about a day longer. His skin's gone past the 'washerwoman' effect, and that suggests he's certainly been in the water more than twenty-four hours. And I'd guess—*guess*, mind!—that we're past the 'sodden' stage and almost up to the time when the skin gets blanched. Let's say about two, two-and-a-half days."

"And nobody would be fool enough to dump him in during the hours of daylight, so—"

"Yep. Sunday night—that's about the time I'd *suggest*, Morse. But if I find a few live fleas on him, it'll mean I'm talking a load of balls; they'd usually be dead after twenty-four hours in the water."

"He doesn't look much like a fellow who had fleas, does he?"

"Depends where he was before they pushed him in. For all we know, he could have been lying in the boot of a car next to a dead dog." He looked across and saw the Chief Inspector looking less than happily into his glass.

"I can understand somebody chopping his head off, Max—even his hands. But why in the name of Sweeney Todd should anyone want to slice his *legs*?"

"Same thing. Identification."

"You mean . . . there was something *below* his knees—couple of wooden legs, or something?"

"'Artificial prostheses,' that's what they call 'em now."

"Or he might have had no toes?"

"Not many of that sort around. . . ."

But Morse's mind was far away, the image of the gruesome corpse producing a further spasm in some section of his gut.

"You're right, you know, Morse!" The surgeon happily poured himself another drink. "He probably wouldn't have *recognized* a flea! Good cut of cloth, that suit. Pretty classy shirt, too. Sort of chap who had a very-nice-job-thank-you: good salary, pleasant conditions of work, carpet all round the office, decent pension. . . ." Suddenly the surgeon broke off, and seemed to arrive at one of his few firm conclusions. "You know what, Morse? I reckon he was probably a bank manager!"

"Or an Oxford don," added Morse quietly.

CHAPTER TEN

Wednesday, 23rd July

In spite of his toothache, Morse begins his investigations with the reconstruction of a letter.

In spite of his unorthodox, intuitive, and seemingly lazy approach to the solving of crime, Morse was an extremely competent administrator; and when he sat down again at his office desk that same evening, all the procedures called for in a case of murder (and this *was* murder) had been, or were about to be, put into effect. Superintendent Strange, to whom Morse had reported on his return to HQ, knew his chief inspector only too well.

"You'll want Lewis, of course?"

"Thank you, sir. Couple of frogmen, too."

"How many extra men?"

"Well—er—none; not for the minute, anyway."

"Why's that?"

"I wouldn't quite know what to ask them to do, sir," had been Morse's simple and honest explanation.

And, indeed, as he looked at his wrist-watch (7:30 p.m.—"Blast, missed *The Archers*!"), he was not at all sure what to ask himself, either. On his desk lay the soddenly promising letter found on the corpse; but his immediate preoccupation was a throbbing toothache which had been getting worse all day. He decided he would do something about it in the morning.

As he sat there, he was conscious that there was a deeper reason for his refusal of the Superintendent's offer of extra personnel. By temperament he was a loner, if only because, although never wholly content in the solitary state, he was almost invariably even more miserable in the company of others. There were a few exceptions, of course, and Lewis was one of them. Exactly why he enjoyed Lewis's company so much, Morse had never really stopped to analyse; but perhaps it was because Lewis was so totally unlike himself. Lewis was placid, good-natured, methodical, honest, unassuming, faithful, and (yes, he might as well come clean about it!) a bit *stolid*, too. Even that afternoon, the good Lewis had been insistently anxious to stay on until whatever hour, if by any chance Morse should consider his availability of any potential value. But Morse had not. As he had pointed out to his sergeant, they *might* pretty soon have a bit of luck and find out who the dead man was; the frogmen *might* just find a few oddments of identifiable limbs in the sludge of the canal waters by Aubrey's Bridge. But Morse doubted it. For, even at this very early stage of the case, he sensed that his major problem would not so much be who the murderer was, *but who exactly had been murdered*. It was Morse's job, though, to find the answer to both these questions; and so he started on his task, alternately stroking his slightly swollen left jaw and prodding down viciously on the offending doublefang. He took the letter lying on the desk in front of him, pressed it very carefully between sheets of blotting-paper, and then removed it. The paper was not so sopped and sodden as he had feared, and with a pair of tweezers he was soon able to unfold a strip about two inches wide and eight inches long. It was immediately apparent that this formed the left-hand side of a typewritten letter; and, furthermore, except for some minor blurring of letters at the torn edge, the message was gladdeningly legible:

Dear Sir,
This is a most unusua
realize. But please re
because what I am pro
both you and me. My wa   5

```
College  has  just  take
final  examinations  in  G
in  about  ten  or  twelve
an  old  man  and  I  am  de
how  she  has  got  on  ah          10
The  reason  for  my  r
ridiculously  impatient
to  America  in  a  few
able  to  be  contacte
what  to  know  how  J          15
this.  I  have  spent  a
education,  and  she  is
I  realize  that  this
only  that  you  should  g
to  such  an  impropriet          20
publication  of  the  cl
July.
If  you  can  possibly  se
shall  be  in  a  positi
unconventionally.  You  s          25
most  select  clubs,  sa
give  you  a  completely
delights  which  area  as
Please  do  give  me  a  r
may  be,  at  01-417  808          30
you  feel  able  to  do
result,  I  shall  give
able  to  enjoy,  at  no  c
the  most  discreet  er
ever  imagined.          35
                    You
```

Morse sat back and studied the words with great joy. He'd been a life-long addict of puzzles and of cryptograms, and this was exactly the sort of work his mind could cope with confidently. First he enumerated the lines in 5's (as shown above); then he set his mind to work. It took him ten minutes, and another ten minutes to copy out his first draft. The general drift of the letter required no Aristotelian intellect to decipher—primarily because of the give-away clue in line 7. But it had been none too easy to concoct some continuum over a few of the individual word-breaks, especially "wa—" in line 5; "ah—" in line 10; "cl—" in line 21; and "sa—" in line 26.

This is the first draft that Morse wrote out:

Dear Sir,

This is a most unusua	l letter as I know you'll
realize. But please re	ad it with great care
because what I am pro	posing can benefit
both you and me. My wa	strel daughter at ——
College has just take	n (without much hope) her
final examinations in G	eography, and will get the result
in about ten or twelve	days' time. Now I am
an old man and I'm de	sperately anxious to know
how she has got on ah	ead of the official lists.
The reason for my r	equest is that I am
ridiculously impatient,	and in fact I am off
to America in a few	days' time where I may not be
able to be contacte	d for some while. All I
want to know is how J	—— got on, if you can tell me
this. I have spent a	great deal of money on her
education, and she is	the only child I have.
I realize that this	is an improper request. I ask
only that you should g	ive a thought to stooping
to such an impropriet	y. I think the official date for
publication of the cl	ass list is —— ——
July.	
If you can possibly se	e your way to this favour,
I shall be in a positi	on to pay you very well, if
unconventionally. You s	ee I manage some of the
most select clubs, sa	unas and parlours and I will
give you a completely	free access to the sexual
delights which are as	sociated with such places.
Please do give me a r	ing, whatever your decision
may be, at 01-417-808	—. If it so happens that
you feel able to do	what I ask about J——'s
result, I shall give	you details about how you'll be
able to enjoy, at no c	ost at all to yourself,
the most discreet er	otic thrills you can have
ever imagined.	

       You   rs sincerely,

Morse was reasonably pleased with the draft. It lacked polish here and there, but it wasn't bad at all, really. Three specific problems, of course: the name of the college, the name of the girl, and the last bit of the telephone number. The college would be a bit more difficult now that almost all of them accepted women, but. . . .

Suddenly Morse sat at his desk quite motionless, the blood tingling across his shoulders. Could it be? That "G—"? It needn't be Geography or Geology or Geo-physics or whatever. And it wasn't. It was *Greats*! and that "J—"? That wasn't Judith or Joanna or Jezebel. It was *Jane*—the girl the Master had indiscreetly mentioned to him! And that would solve the college automatically; it was *Lonsdale*!

Phew!

The telephone number wouldn't be much of a problem, either, since Lewis could soon sort that out. If it was a four-digit group, that would only mean ten possibilities; and if it was five-digits, that was only a hundred, and Lewis was a very patient man. . . .

But the tooth was jabbing its pain along his jaw once more, and he made his way home, where doubling (as he invariably did) the dosage of all medical nostrums he took six Aspros, washed them down well with whisky, and went to bed. But at 2 a.m. we find him sitting up in bed, his hand caressing his jaw, the pain jumping in his gum like some demented dervish. And at 8 a.m. we find him standing outside a deserted dentist's premises in North Oxford, an inordinately long scarf wrapped round his jaw, waiting desperately for one of the receptionists to arrive.

CHAPTER ELEVEN

Thursday, 24th July

Wherein such diverse activities as dentistry, crossword-solving, and pike-angling make their appropriate contributions to Morse's view of things.

"You've not been looking after these too well, have you, Mr. Morse?"

Since at this point, however, the dapperly-dressed dentist had his patient's mouth opened to its widest extremities, Morse was able only to produce a strained grunt from his swollen larynx.

"You ought to cut out the sugar," continued the dentist, surveying so many signs of incipient decay, "and some dental-floss wouldn't come amiss with all this. . . . Ah! I reckon that's the little fellow that's been causing you—" He tapped one of the lower-left molars with a blunt instrument, and the recumbent Morse was almost levitated in agony. "Ye-es, you've got a nasty little infection there . . . does *that* hurt?"

Again Morse's body jumped in agonizing pain, before the chair was raised to a semi-vertical slant and he was ordered to "rinse out."

"You've got a nasty little infection there, as I say. . . ."

Everything with the dentist appeared to warrant the epithet "little," and Morse would have been more gratified had it been suggested to him that he was the victim of a massive great bloody infection stemming from an equally massive great bloody tooth that even now was throbbing

65

mightily. He continued to sit in the chair, but the dentist himself was writing something across at his desk.

"Aren't you going to take it out?" asked Morse.

The dentist continued writing. "We try to preserve as many teeth as we can these days, you know. And it's particularly important for *you* not to lose many more. You haven't got too many left, have you?"

"But it's giving me—"

"Here's a prescription for a little pencillin. Don't worry! It'll soon sort out the infection and get that little swelling down. Then if you come and see me again in—a week, shall we say?"

"A *week*?"

"I can't do anything till then. If I took it out now— well, let's say you'd have to be a brave man, Mr. Morse."

"Would I?" said Morse weakly. He finally rose from the chair, and his eyes wandered to the shelf of plaster-casts of teeth behind the dentist's desk, the upper jaws resting on the lower, a few canines missing here, a few molars there. It all seemed rather obscene to Morse, and reminded him of his junior-school history books, with their drawings of skulls labelled with such memorable names as *Eoanthropus dawsoni*, *Pithecanthropus erectus*, and the rest.

The dentist saw his interest and reached down a particularly ugly cast, snapping the jaws apart and together again like a ventriloquist at a dumb-show. "Remarkable things teeth, you know. No two sets of teeth can ever be the same. Each set—well, it's unique, like finger-prints." He looked at the squalid lump of plastering with infinite compassion, and it seemed quite obvious that teeth obsessed not only his working life but his private soul as well.

Morse stood beside him, waiting for the prescription; and when the dentist got to his feet Morse became surprisingly aware of how small a man the dentist was. Had it been the white coat that had given him the semblance of being taller? Had it been the fact that the last thing Morse had earlier been interested in was whether the kindly man who'd readily agreed to see one of his most irregular clients was a dwarf or a giant? Yet there was something else, wasn't there?

Morse's mind suddenly grasped it as he stood waiting at the Summertown chemist's. It had been when the dentist had been sitting at his desk—yes. Because the length of his back was that of a man of normal height; and so it must have been *the legs*. . . .

"Are you a pensioner, sir?" asked the young assistant as she took his prescription. (My God! Could he really look as old as that?)

After an exhortation to stick religiously to the stated dosage, and also to be sure to complete the course, Morse was soon on his way to Kidlington, quite convinced now of the perfectly obvious fact that whoever had dismembered the corpse had been at desperate pains to conceal its identity.

Teeth? The murderer would have left a means of certain identification—"unique," as his little torturer had said. Hands? If they had been deformed in any way, or one of them had? It was difficult for fellow humans to forget deformity. Legs? What if that exciting idea that had occurred to him at the chemist's. . . .

But he was at HQ now, and the need for instant action was at hand. He swallowed twice the specified dosage of tablets, told himself that the marvellous stuff was already engaged in furious conflict with the "little infection," and finally greeted Lewis at 9:30 a.m.

"You said you'd be here by eight, sir."

"You're lucky to see me at all!" Morse snapped, as he unwrapped his scarf and bared his bulging jaw.

"Bad tooth, sir?"

"Not just *bad*, Lewis, It's the worst bloody tooth in England!"

"The missus always swears by—"

"Forget what your missus says! She's not a dentist, is she?"

So Lewis forgot it, and sat down silently.

Soon Morse was feeling better, and for an hour he discussed with Lewis both the letter and the curious thoughts that had been occurring to him.

"Someone certainly seems to be making it difficult for us," said Lewis; and the sentence did little more than state in simple English the even simpler thought that had gradually dawned on Morse's mind. But for Lewis life was full of surprises, since he now heard Morse ask him to repeat exactly that same sentence. And as he did so, Lewis saw the familiar sight of his chief looking out over the concreted yard, or wherever it was those eyes, unblinking, stared with more than a hint of deeper understanding.

"Or it could be just the opposite," Lewis heard him mumble enigmatically.

"Pardon, sir?"

"Do you reckon a cup of coffee would upset this tooth of mine?"

"Be all right, unless it's too hot."

"Nip and get a couple of cups."

After Lewis had gone, Morse unfolded *The Times* and looked at the crossword. 1 across: "He lived perched up, mostly in sites around East, shivering (6,8)." Anagram, obviously: "mostly in sites" round "e." Yes! He quickly wrote in "Simon Stylites"—only to find himself one letter short. Of course! It was *Simeon* Stylites, and he was about to correct the letters, when he stopped.

It *couldn't* be, surely!

He wrote a circle of letters in the bottom margin of the newspaper, crossed off a few letters, then a few more—and stopped again. Not only could it be, it was! What an extraordinary—

"I told her to stick some extra cold milk in, sir."

"Did you sugar it?"

"You do take sugar, don't you?"

"Bad for the teeth—surely you know that?"

"Shall I go and—"

"No—siddown. I've got something to show you. Oh God! This coffee's cold!"

"You haven't done much of the crossword."

"Haven't I?" Morse was smiling serenely, and he thrust the paper across to Lewis who looked down uncomprehendingly at the almost illegible alterations in the top row of squares. But Lewis was happy. The chief was on to something—the chief was always on to something, and that was good. That's why he enjoyed working with Morse. Being on the receiving end of all the unpredictability, all the irascibility, all the unfairness—it was a cheap price to pay for working with him. And now he whistled softly to himself as Morse explained the riddle of the circle of letters he had printed.

"Do you want me to get on to it, sir?"

"No, I'd rather you got on with those telephone numbers."

"Straightaway, you mean?"

Morse gestured gently towards the phone on his desk, a smile spreading lopsidedly across his swollen mouth. "You said it was Dickson on the desk yesterday when we got the call from Thrupp?"

"Yes."

"Well, you get on with things here, Lewis. I'm just going to have a little chat with Dickson."

If Lewis's weakness in life was the smell of freshly-fried chips (and fast driving!), with Dickson it was the sight of amply-jammed doughnuts, and he sought to swallow his latest mouthful hastily as he saw Morse bearing down on him.

"Fingers a bit sticky this morning, Dickson?"

"Sorry, sir."

"Sugar is bad for the teeth, didn't you know that?"

"Do you eat a lot yourself, sir?"

For the next few minutes Morse questioned Dickson patiently about the informant who had telephoned HQ about the corpse in the water by Aubrey's Bridge. The facts were clear. The man had not only given his name, he'd spelt it out; he hadn't been absolutely sure that what he had seen was a human body, but it most decidedly looked like one; the call had been made from a phone-box, and after the second lot of "pip-pips" the line had gone dead.

"*Is* there a phone-box in Thrupp?"

"On the corner, by the pub, sir."

Morse nodded. "Did it not occur to you, my lad, that after getting this fellow's name you ought to have got his *address*? In the book of rules, isn't it?"

"Yes, sir, but—"

"Why didn't he want to keep talking, tell me that."

"Probably ran out of 10p's."

"He could have rung you again later."

"Probably thought he'd—he'd already done his duty."

"More than you did, eh?"

"Yes, sir."

"Why didn't he stay there at Thrupp?"

"Not everybody likes seeing—sort of drowned people."

Morse conceded the point, and moved on. "What do they fish for there?"

"They say there's a few biggish pike up by the bridge."

"Really? Who the hell's 'they'?"

"Well, one of my lads, sir. He's been fishing for pike up there a few times."

"Keen fisherman, is he?"

Dickson was feeling more at ease now. "Yes, sir, he's joined the Oxford Pike Anglers' Association."

"I see. Is the fellow who rang you up a member, too?"

Dickson swallowed hard. "I don't know, sir."

"Well, bloody well find out, will you!"

Morse walked away a few steps from the flustered Dickson; then he walked back. "And I'll tell you something else, lad. If your man Rowbotham *is* a member of whatever it's called, I'll buy you every bloody doughnut in the canteen. And that's a promise!"

Morse walked over to the canteen, ordered another cup of coffee with plenty of milk, smoked a cigarette, assessed the virulence of his gnathic bacteria, noted the pile of approximately thirty-five doughnuts on the counter, and returned to his office.

It was Lewis who was beaming with pleasure now. "Got it, I reckon, sir!" He showed Morse the list he made. "Only four digits and so they're only the ten numbers. What do you think?"

Morse read the list:

8080—J. Pettiford, Tobacconist, Piccadilly
8081—Comprehensive Assurance Co., Shaftes-
          bury Avenue

8082—ditto

8083—ditto

8084—Douglas Schwartz, Reproductions, Old
      Compton Street

8085—Ping Hong Restaurant, Brewer Street

8086—Claude & Mathilde, Unisex Hairdressers,
      Lower Regent Street

8087—Messrs. Levi & Goldstein, Antiquarian
      Books, Tottenham Court Road

8088—The Flamenco Topless Bar, Soho Terrace

"There's one missing, Lewis."

"You want me to—?"

"I told you to try them all, I think."

But whoever was renting number 8089 was clearly away from base, and Morse told Lewis to forget it.

"We are not, my friend, exactly driving through the trackless wastes of the Sahara with a broken axle, you agree? Now, if you can just make one more call and find out the price of a cheap-day second-class return to Paddington—"

"Are we going there?"

"Well, one of us'll have to, Lewis, and it's important for you to stay here, isn't it, because I've got one or two very interesting little things I want you to look into. So I'll—er—perhaps go myself."

"It won't do your tooth much good."

"Ah! That reminds me," said Morse. "I think it's about time I took another pill or two."

CHAPTER TWELVE

Thursday, 24th July

A brief interlude in which Sergeant Lewis takes his first steps into the Examination Schools, the Moloch of Oxford's testing apparatus.

It was late morning when, from its frontage on The High, Sergeant Lewis entered the high-roofed, hammer-beamed lobby of the Examination Schools. Never before had there been occasion for him to visit this grove of Academe, and he felt self-conscious as his heavy boots echoed over the mosaics of the marble floor, patterned in green and blue and orange. At intervals, in front of the oak-panelling that lined the walls, were stationed the white and less-than-animated busts of former University Chancellors, former loyal servants of the monarchy, and sundry other benefactors. And along the walls themselves was a series of "faculty" headings: Theology, Philosophy, Oriental Studies, Modern History, and the rest; below which, behind glass, were pinned a line of notices announcing the names of those candidates adjudged to have satisfied, in varying degrees, the appropriate panels of the faculties' examiners.

On the *Literae Humaniores* ("Greats") board (as Morse had assured him he would) Lewis duly found a long list of names, categorized into Class I, Class II, Class III, and Pass Degree. He noticed, too (as Morse had assured him he would), that a young lady by the name of Summers (Jane) of Lonsdale College, had secured a place in the first of these aforesaid categories. Then, doing precisely as he had been told, Lewis looked to the bottom of the list, where he saw the signatures of seven examiners. A few of them were barely legible. But one of them was conspicuously clear: the neatly penned signature of O. M. A. Browne-Smith. So Lewis made a brief entry in his notebook, and wondered why Morse had bothered to send him on this particular errand.

An attendant was seated in an office to the left of the lobby, and Lewis was soon enlisting this man's ready assistance in learning something of the processes involved in the evolution of the class-lists. What happened, it seemed, was this. After candidates had finished their written examinations, mark coordination meetings were held by each of the examining panels, where "classes" were provisionally allotted, and where borderline candidates at each class-boundary were considered for vivas, especially those candidates hovering between a first and a second; finally, but then only the day before the definitive lists were due to be published, the chairman of the examiners (and no one else) was fully in possession of all the facts. At that point it was the duty of the chairman of examiners to summon his colleagues together in order to make a corporate, meticulous check of the final lists, and then to entrust the agreed document to one of the senior personnel of the Schools, whose task it now was to deliver the document for printing to the Oxford University Press. Immediately this was done, five copies of the lists were re-delivered to the waiting panel, who would usually be sitting around drinking tea and eating a few sandwiches during the hour or so's interval. There would follow the long and tedious checking of all results, the spellings of names, and the details of index-numbers and colleges, before the chairman would read aloud to his colleagues the final version, down to the last diaeresis and comma. Only then, if all were correct, would the chairman summon the Clerk of the Schools, in whose august presence each of the five copies would be signed in turn by each of the examiners. Then, at long last, the master-copy would be posted in the lobby of the Schools.

Lewis thanked the attendant, and clattered out across the entrance hall, where examinees, parents, and friends were still clustered eagerly round the notice-boards. For the first time in his life he felt a little envy for those white-tied, subfusc-suited students so happily perched upon the topmost boughs of the tree of knowledge. But such thoughts were futile. Anyway, he had his second assignment ahead of him—at the Churchill Hospital.

Morse was out when he returned, and so for a change it was Lewis who had some little time in which to ponder how the case was going. On the whole, he thought that Morse was probably right. Far from being stranded in the Sahara, they were following a fairly well-directed route, with signposts at almost all the early stages—quite certainly at the Examination Schools; but not (Lewis reminded himself) at the Churchill, where his enquiries had yielded nothing, and where Morse's confident predictions had clearly gone dramatically askew.

CHAPTER
THIRTEEN

Thursday, 24th July

Quite fortuitously, Morse lights upon a set of college rooms which he had no original intention of visiting.

Morse himself had decided to postpone for a day or two the pleasures of a trip to Soho, and instead to make some more immediate enquiries in Oxford. Thus it is that just before midday he was parking the Lancia in one of the spaces at the back of Lonsdale ("Reserved for Senior Fellows"), walking through the front gate ("No Visitors"), and introducing himself at the Lodge. Here, a bowler-hatted porter, very young but already equipped with the requisite blend of servility and officiousness, was perfectly willing to answer the questions Morse put to him: yes, most of the undergrads had now gone down for the long vac; yes, most of the dons had also departed, amongst their number the Master, the Vice-Master, the Investments Bursar, the Domestic Bursar, the Senior Tutor, the Senior Fellow, the. . . .

"Off to the Bahamas, all of them?"

"Continent mostly, sir—and Greece."

"You think it's all those topless beaches, perhaps?"

For a few seconds the young porter leered as though he were about to produce a dirty postcard from one of the innumerable pigeon-holes, but he quickly resumed his dignity. "I wouldn't know about that, sir."

"What about Dr. Browne-Smith? Is he still away?"

"I've not seen him in college since we had a note from him . . . and then we had a—just a minute." He went over

to his desk and returned to the "Enquiries" window with a
sheaf of papers. In spite of having to read them upside-
down, Morse was able to read some of the messages clearly:
"Professor M. Liebermann—back 6th August. All post to
Pension Heimstadt, Friederichstrasse 14, Zurich"; "Mr. G.
Westerby—off to Greece until end of August. Keep all mail
at the Lodge"; "Dr. Browne-Smith. . . ."

"Here we are, sir."

Morse took the handwritten sheet and read the few
words: "Away untill further notice no forwarding adress."
Mentally deleting an "l," inserting a "d," and introducing a
major stop into mid-message, Morse handed the sheet
back. "Phone message, was it?"

"Yes, sir. Yesterday, I think it was—or Tuesday."

"You took it yourself?"

The porter nodded.

"It was Dr. Browne-Smith who rang?"

"I think so, yes."

"You know him well?"

The young man shrugged. "Pretty well."

"You'd recognize his voice all right?"

"Well—"

"How long have you been here?"

"More than three months now."

"Just let me have the key to his rooms, will you?"
Morse pointed peremptorily to a bunch of keys hanging
beside the pigeon-holes, and the porter did as he was
told.

The book-lined room to which Morse admitted himself
was shady and silent as the grave. Everywhere there were
signs of the academic pursuits to which Browne-Smith had
devoted his life: on the desk, a large stack of typescript of
what appeared to be a forthcoming opus on Philip, father of
Alexander the Great, and scores of photographs, slides, and
postcards; on a bookcase beside the desk a marble bust of a
sombre-featured Cicero; on the few square yards of the
walls still free from books, many black-and-white photographs of temples, vases and statuary. But nothing un-
toward; nothing out of place.

Leading off this main room were two other rooms: one a bleakish-looking, rather dirty WC; the other a small bedroom, containing a single bed, hundreds more books, a white wash-basin and a large mahogany wardrobe. The door of the wardrobe creaked noisily as Morse opened it and looked vaguely along the line of suits and shirts. He told himself he should have brought a tape-measure, but he accepted the fact that usually such forward-planning was quite beyond him. Apart from patting a few pockets, his only other interest appeared to lie in a very large selection of socks, whence he abstracted a brand-new pair and stuffed them in his pocket.

Back in the main room, his eyes wandered along the shelves and into the alcoves (failing to observe the small cooking-ring); but again he seemed mildly satisfied. He picked up a virgin sheet of paper, flicked it into the portable typewriter which stood beside the typescript, and clumsily tapped his way through the leap of the lazy, brown fox over the something or other. Morse couldn't quite remember it all, but he knew he'd got most of the letters included.

As he closed the door beind him (forgetting to re-lock it), he felt a few more sudden jabs in his lower jaw; and, although that unsettled July had at last turned hot and sunny, he pulled his scarf round his throat once more as he stood on the wide, wooden landing. He looked around him, first up the stairs, then down them; then across to the room immediately opposite, where the name G. D. Westerby was printed above the door. Yes! He had seen that name ten minutes ago in the Porters' Lodge; and the owner of that name was, at that very moment, sunning himself on some Aegean island, surely. Yet the door stood slightly open, and Morse stepped silently across the landing and listened.

There was someone there. For a few seconds Morse felt a childlike shudder of fear, but only (he told himself) because of his recent prying in the quiet rooms behind him. Anyway, it would only be some staircase-scout doing a bit of tidying up, dusting. . . . But suddenly the rustling noises ceased, succeeded by the more reassuring clean-cut metallic clacks of hammer upon nails; and Morse felt better. Pushing open the door he saw a room very similar to the one he had just left, except that tea-chests and packing crates (most of them with address labels already attached) were bestrewn over almost the whole of the carpet-area, in the midst of which a youth of no more than sixteen or seventeen, dressed in a khaki overall, was inexpertly fixing a lid to one of the wooden crates. As Morse came in, the youth looked up; but only it seemed from curiosity, for he promptly returned to his amateurish bangings.

"Excuse me, is Mr.—er—Westerby in?"

"On holiday, I think," said the spotty-faced youth.

"I'm—er—one of his colleagues. I was very much hoping to catch him before he went." This explanation appeared unworthy of further comment, for the youth merely nodded and drove yet another nail askew into the wooden lath.

Almost exactly the same layout of rooms as opposite— even the similar positioning of the working desk, with a similar pile of typescript, and exactly the same model of portable typewriter. And Morse knew in a flash what he was about to do, although he had almost no idea of why he did it.

"I'll just leave a note for him, lad, if you'll let me through."

From his pocket he took out the sheet he had just typed, and put the lazy, brown fox through his faltering paces once more.

"Your firm's moving the old boy, I see."

"Yeah."

"Lot of stuff—he always kept a lot of stuff."

"Books!" (Clearly the youth had as yet no great respect for literature.)

The crate that was in the process of being lidded was doubtless packed with objects that were eminently breakable, since three-quarters of its contents appeared to be wrapped in crumpled newspaper. And there was another crate, alongside, presumably designated for a similar purpose, with a battalion of cut-glass objects, still unwrapped, surrounding it on the carpet. But other objects had already been deposited in this second crate—bulkier objects; and one in particular that lay snugly in the middle, swathed in past editions of *The Times*. It was about the shape of a

medium-sized goldfish bowl, almost the size of a—yes!—
almost the size of a head.

"I'm glad to see you're being careful with the old boy's
valuables," Morse heard himself saying as he knelt down
beside this crate and, with a shaking hand, touched the
packaged article, where his probing fingers soon felt the
configurations of a human nose and a human mouth.

"What's this?" he managed to ask.

The youth looked across at him. "Mr. Gilbert told me
to be very careful about that."

"Who's Mr. Gilbert?"

"*I'm* Mr. Gilbert!"

Morse almost panicked as he turned to the door and
saw a man of about sixty, perhaps—grey-flannelled and
shirt-sleeved, with a pair of gold-rimmed, half-glasses on
his nose, and a pair of no-nonsense eyes behind them. But
there was something else about him—the first thing that
anyone would notice: for, like Morse, he wore a scarf that
draped his lower jaw.

"Hullo, Mr. Gilbert. I'm—ah—one of Westerby's colleagues here. He asked me to look in from time to time to
see, you know, that the stuff was being stowed away carefully."

"We're looking after that all right, sir."

"He's got some valuable things here—"

"Have no fears, sir! We're looking after everything
beautifully." With agility he picked his way across the room
and stood above the still-kneeling Morse. "You know we get
more fusspots in this business, especially with the
women—"

"But some of this stuff—well, you just couldn't replace
it, could you?"

"No?" Mr. Gilbert's tone sounded too knowledgeable
for Morse to demur. "I'll tell you one thing, sir. Almost all
my clients would prefer to collect their insurance money."

"Perhaps so." Morse rose to his feet, and as he did so
Gilbert's shrewd eyes seemed to measure him for crating,
like some melancholy undertaker surveying a corpse for cof-
fining. "It's just that he asked me—"

"Look around and check up, sir! We're only too anxious to give every satisfaction—aren't we, Charlie?"

The young assistant nodded. "Yes, Mr. Gilbert."

Almost involuntarily Morse's eyes were drawn down once again to the head in the unlidded crate, and Gilbert's eyes were following.

"He's all right. Don't worry about him, sir. Took us a good ten minutes to put him to bed."

"What is it?" asked Morse weakly.

"You want me to—?" There was annoyance in Gilbert's face.

Morse nooded.

If it had taken ten minutes to put this particular valuable finally to rest, it took less than ten seconds to resurrect it. And it *was* a head, a marble head of Gerardus Mercator, the Flemish geographer—a head chopped off at the neck, like the head of the man who had been dragged from the canal out at Thrupp.

A somewhat foolish-looking Morse now hastened to take his leave, but before doing so he sought briefly to mitigate the awkward little episode. He addressed himself to Gilbert: "You a fellow sufferer, I see."

For a second or two Gilbert's eyes looked puzzled—suspicious almost. "Ah—the scarf—yes! Abscess. But the dentist won't touch it. What about you, sir?"

So Morse told him, and the two men chatted amiably enough for a couple of minutes. Then Morse departed.

From the window, Gilbert watched Morse as he walked towards the Lodge.

"How the hell did he get in?"

"I must have left the door open."

"Well, you're going to have to learn to keep doors *shut* in this business—understand? One of the first rules of the trade, that is. Still, you've not been with us long, have you?"

"Month." The youth looked surly, and Gilbert's tone was deliberately softer as he continued.

"Never mind—no harm done. You don't know who he is, do you?"

"No. But I saw him go into the room opposite, then I heard him come out again."

"Opposite, eh?" Gilbert opened the door, and looked out. "Mm. That must be Dr. Browne-Smith, then."

"He said he was a friend o' this fellah here."

"Well, you believed him, didn't you?"

"Yeah—'course."

"As I say, though, we can't be too careful in this job, Charlie. Lots of valuables around. It's always the same."

"He didn't take anything."

"No, I'm sure he didn't. He—er—just sort of looked round, you say?"

"Yeah, looked around a bit—said he wanted to leave a message for this fellah, that's all."

"Where's the message?" Gilbert's voice was suddenly sharp.

"I dunno. He just typed—"

"He *what*?"

The unhappy Charlie pointed vaguely to the portable. "He just typed a little note on that thing, that's all."

"Ah, I see. Well, if that's all—" Gilbert's face seemed to relax, and his tone was kindly again. "But look, my lad. If you're going to make a success of this business, you've got to be a bit cagey, like me. When you're moving people, see, it's easy as a wink for someone to nip in the property and pretend he's a relative or something. Then he nicks all the silver—and then where are we? Understand?"

"Yeah."

"So. Let's start being cagey right away, OK? You be a good lad, and just nip down to the Lodge, and see if they know who that fellow was in here. It'll be a bit of good experience for you."

Without enthusiasm, Charlie went out, and for a second time Gilbert walked over to the window, and waited until the young apprentice was out of sight. Then he put on a pair of working gloves, picked up the portable typewriter and crossed the landing. He knew that the door opposite was unlocked (since he had already tried it on his way up), and very swiftly he entered the room and exchanged the typewriter he carried for the one on Dr. Browne-Smith's desk.

Gilbert was kneeling by one of the crates, carefully re-packing the head of Gerardus Mercator, when a rather worried-looking Charlie returned.

"It was the *police*."

"Really?" Gilbert kept his eyes on his work. "Well, that's good news. Somebody must have seen you here and thought the college had a burglar or something. Yes—that explains it. You see, lad, there aren't many people in the colleges this time of year. They've nearly all gone, so it's a good time for burglars, understand?"

Charlie nodded, and was soon attaching an address label to the recently-lidded crate: G. D. Westerby, Esq., Flat 6, 29 Cambridge Way, London, WC1.

CHAPTER
FOURTEEN

Thursday, 24th July

*Preliminary investigations are now in full swing,
and Morse appears unconcerned about the con-
tradictory evidence that emerges.*

It might perhaps appear to the reader that Morse had
come off slightly the worse in the exchanges recorded in the
previous chapter. But the truth is that after a late pub lunch
Morse returned to his office exceedingly satisfied with his
morning's work, since fresh ideas were breeding in profusion now.

He was still seated there, deep in thought, when three
quarters of an hour later the phone rang. It was the police
surgeon.

"Look, I'll cut out the technicalities. You can read 'em in
my report—and anyway you wouldn't be able to follow 'em.
Adult, male, Caucasian; sixtyish or slightly more; well nourished; no signs of any physical abnormality; pretty healthy
except for the lungs, but there's no tumour there—in fact
there's no tumour or neoplasm anywhere—we don't call it
cancer these days, you know. By the way, you still smoking,
Morse?"

"Get on with it!"

"Dead before immersion—"

"You *do* surprise me."

"—and probably curled up a bit after death."

"He was carried there, you mean?"

"I said 'probably.'"

"In the boot of a car?"

"How the hell do I know!"

"Anything else?"

"Dismembered *after* death—pretty certain of that."

"Brilliant," mumbled Morse.

"And that's almost it, old man."

Morse was secretly delighted with these findings, but for the moment he feigned a tone of disappointment. "But aren't you going to tell me *how* he died? That's what they pay you for, isn't it?"

As ever, the surgeon sounded unperturbed. "Tricky question, that. No obvious wounds—or unobvious ones for that matter. Somebody could have clobbered him about the head—a common enough cause of death, as well you know. But we haven't *got* a head, remember?"

"Not poisoned?" asked Morse more quietly.

"Don't think so. It's never all that easy to tell when you've got your giblets soaked in water."

"Didn't you bother to have a look at his guts?"

"Ah, yes. Drop of Scotch there, Morse. But, after all, there's a drop of Scotch in most—By the way, Morse, you still boozing?"

"I've not quite managed to cut it out."

"And some kippers. You interested in kippers?"

"For breakfast?"

"He'd had some, yes. But whether he'd had 'em for breakfast—"

"You mean he might have had the Scotch for breakfast and the kippers for lunch?"

"We live in a strange world."

"Nothing else?"

"As I said, that's almost the lot."

With huge self-gratification, Morse now prepared to launch his Exocet. "Well, thanks very much, Max. But if I may say so I reckon somebody at your end—I'm sure it isn't you!—deserves a hefty kick up the arse. As you know, I don't pretend to be a pathologist myself but—"

"I said it was 'almost' the lot, Morse, and I know what you're going to say. I just thought I'd leave it to the end—you know, just to humour an old friend and all that."

"It's that bloody *arm* I'm talking about!"

"Yes, yes! I know that. You just hold your horses a minute! I noticed you looking down at that arm, of course, almost as if you thought you'd made some wonderful discovery. Discovery? What? With that bloody great bruise there? You don't honestly think even a part-time hospital-porter could have missed that, do you?"

Morse growled his discomfiture down the phone, and the surgeon proceeded placidly.

"Funny thing, Morse. You just *happened* to be right in what you thought—not for the right reasons, though. That contusion on the left arm, it was nothing to do with giving blood. He must have just knocked himself somewhere—or somebody else knocked *him*. But you were right, he *was* a blood donor. Difficult to be certain, but I examined his arms very carefully and I reckon he'd probably had the needle about twenty to twenty-five times in his left arm; about twelve to fifteen in his right."

"Mm." For a few seconds Morse was silent. "Send me the full report over, please, Max."

"It won't help much."

"*I'll* decide that, thank you very much."

"What do I do with the corpse?"

"Put it in the bloody deep-freeze!"

A few mintues later, after slamming down the phone, Morse rang Lonsdale and asked for the college secretary.

"Can I help you?" She had a nice voice, but for once it didn't register with Morse.

"Yes! I want to know whether the college had kippers for breakfast on Friday, 11th July."

"I don't know. I could try to find out, I suppose."

"Well, *find* out!" snapped Morse.

"Can I ring you back, sir?" She was obviously distressed, but Morse was crudely adamant.

"No! Do it now!"

Morse heard a hectic, whispered conversation at the other end of the line, and eventually a male voice, defensive but quite firm, took over.

"Andrews, here. Perhaps *I* could help you, inspector."

And, indeed, he could; for he happened to live with his family in Kidlington, and professed himself only too glad to call in at police HQ later that same afternoon.

Lewis, who had come in during this latter call, realized immediately that someone had seriously upset the chief, and he was not at all hopeful about how his own two items of information would be received—especially the second. But Morse appeared surprisingly amiable and listened attentively as Lewis recounted what he had learned at the Examination Schools.

"So you see, sir," he concluded, "no one, not even the chairman, could be absolutely certain of all the results until just before the final list goes up."

Morse just nodded, and sat back almost happily.

But Lewis had barely begun his report on his second visit when Morse sat forward and exploded.

"You couldn't have looked carefully enough, Lewis! Of course he's bloody there!"

"But he's not, sir. I checked and re-checked everything—so did the girl."

"Didn't it occur to you they'd probably put him under 'Smith' or something?"

Lewis replied quietly: "If you really want to know, I looked under 'Brown,' and 'Browne' with an 'e'; and 'Smith,' and 'Smithe' with an 'e'; and I looked through all the rest of the 'B's and the 'S's just in case his card was out of order. But you'd better face it, sir. Unless they've lost his records, *Dr. Browne-Smith isn't a blood donor at all.*"

"Oh!" For some time Morse just sat there, and then he smiled. "Why didn't you try under the 'W's?"

"Pardon?"

"Forget it! For the minute anyway. Now let me tell you a few interesting facts."

So Morse, in turn, recounted his own morning's work, and finished up by handing over to Lewis the sheet of paper on which he had typed his two sentences.

"See that second one, Lewis?"

Lewis nodded as he looked down at the version beginning "The laxy brown fox 13aped. . . ."

"Well, that's the same typewriter as the one used for the letter we found on the body!"

Lewis whistled in genuine amazement. "You're sure you're not mistaken, sir?"

"Lew-is!" (The eyes were almost frighteningly unblinking once more.) "And there's something else." He pushed across the desk the note that the Master of Lonsdale had given him earlier—the note supposedly left in the Porters' Lodge by Browne-Smith. "*That* was done on the same typewriter, too!"

"Whew!"

"So your next job—"

"Just a minute, sir. You're quite certain, are you, which typewriter it was?"

"Oh yes, Lewis. *It was Westerby's.*"

He was very happy now, and looked across at Lewis with the satisfaction of a man leaning over the parapet of infallibility.

So it was that Lewis was forthwith despatched to impound the two typewriters, whilst Morse took two more penicillin tablets and waited for the arrival of Mr. Andrews, Ancient History Tutor of Lonsdale.

CHAPTER FIFTEEN

Thursday, 24th July

From two sources, Morse gains valuable insight into the workings of the human mind, and specifically into the mind of Dr. Browne-Smith of Lonsdale.

Andrews ("a good young man," as Browne-Smith had earlier described him) turned out to be about Morse's age—a slim, bespectacled, shrewd-looking man of medium height who gave the immediate impression of not suffering fools at all gladly. For the time being he was (as he told Morse) the senior resident fellow at Lonsdale, in which capacity he was far from happy about the way the college secretary had been telephonically assaulted. But, yes: on Friday, 11th July, the college had breakfasted on kippers. That had been the question—and that was the answer.

So Morse began to like the man, and was soon telling him about the Master's mild anxiety over Browne-Smith, as well as about his own involvement in the matter.

"Let me come clean, inspector. I know more about this than you think. Before he left, the Master told *me* he was worried about Browne-Smith."

"If he's got any sense, he's *still* worried."

"But we had a note from him."

"Which he didn't write."

"Can you prove that?" Andrews asked, as if prodding some semi-informed student into producing a piece of textual evidence.

"Browne-Smith's dead, I'm afraid, sir."

For a few moments Andrews sat silently, his eyes betraying no sense of shock or surprise.

"Was he a blood donor?" asked Morse suddenly.

"I don't know. Not the sort of thing one broadcasts, would you say?"

"Some people have those 'Give Blood' stickers on the car windows."

"I don't remember seeing—"

"Did he have a car?"

"Big, black, thirsty Daimler."

"Where's that now?"

"I've no idea."

"What was his favourite tipple in the Common Room?"

"He liked a drop of Scotch, as most of us do, but he wasn't a big drinker. He was an Aristotelian, inspector; with him it was always the half-way house between the too much and the too little—if you—er—follow what I'm saying."

"Yes, I think I do."

"You remember the Cambridge story that Trinity once saw Wordsworth drunk and once saw Porson sober? Well, I can tell you one thing: Lonsdale never once saw Browne-Smith drunk."

"He was a bore, you mean?"

"I mean nothing of the sort. It's just that he couldn't abide woolly-mindedness, shoddiness, carelessness—"

"He wouldn't have made too many mistakes in English grammar?"

"Over his dead body!"

"Which is precisely where we stand, sir," said Morse sombrely.

Andrews waited a moment or two. "You really are quite sure of that?"

"He's dead," repeated Morse flatly. "His body was fished out of the canal up at Thrupp yesterday."

Morse was conscious of the steady, scholarly eyes upon him as Andrews spoke: "But I only read about that in the *Oxford Mail* this lunchtime. It said the body couldn't be identified."

"Really?" Morse appeared genuinely surprised. "Surely you don't believe everything you read in the newspapers, sir?"

"No, but I believe most of it," replied Andrews simply and tellingly; and Morse abruptly switched his questioning.

"Dr. Browne-Smith, sir. Was he a fit man—considering his age, I mean?"

For the first time Andrews appeared less than completely at ease. "You know something about that?"

"Well, not officially, but . . ."

Andrews stared down at the threadbare carpet. "Look, inspector, the only reason the Master mentioned anything to me . . ."

"Go on!"

". . . well, it's because I shall be taking over his duties in the College, you see."

"After he retires?"

"Or before, I'm afraid. You—er—you knew, didn't you, that he'd only a few months to live?"

Morse nodded, quite convincingly.

"Tragic thing, inspector—cancer of the brain."

Morse shook his head. "You're as bad as the Master, sir. 'Cancer?' Forget the word! 'Tumour,' if you like—or 'neoplasm.' They're the generic terms we use these days for all those nasty things we used to call 'cancer.'" (He congratulated himself on remembering the gist of what the surgeon had told him earlier that afternoon.)

"I'm not a medical man myself, inspector."

"Nor me, really. But, you know, in this job you have to pick up a few things, sometimes. By the way, are you likely yourself to be much better off—financially, I mean—with Dr. Browne-Smith out of the way?"

"What the hell's *that* supposed to mean?"

"It means we're dealing with murder, that's all," said Morse, looking across the table with guileless eyes. "And that's what they pay me for, sir—trying to find out who murdered people."

"All right. If you must know, I shall be just over two thousand a year better off."

"You're gradually shinning up the tree, sir."

"Not so gradually, either!" Andrews' eyes glinted momentarily with the future prospects of further academic preferment, and momentarily Morse was taken aback by the honesty of his answer.

"But the Master's still got about ten years to go," objected Morse.

"Eight actually."

Strangely, this was neither an unpleasant nor an embarrassing moment, as though each man had perfectly understood and perfectly respected the other's thoughts.

"Head of House!" said Morse slowly. "Great honour, isn't it?"

"For me it's always seemed the greatest honour."

"Do most of the dons share your view?"

"Most of them—if they're honest."

"Did Browne-Smith?"

"Oh, quite certainly, yes."

"So he was a disappointed man?"

"Life's full of disappointments, inspector."

Morse nodded. "Had Browne-Smith any physical abnormalities you can remember?"

"Don't think so—except for his finger, of course. He lost most of his right index-finger—accident in the war. But you probably know all about that."

Morse nodded, again quite convincingly. God, he'd forgotten all about that! And suddenly the hooked atoms were engaging and re-engaging themselves so rapidly in his mind that he was desperately anxious to rid himself of the worthy man seated opposite who had put the fire to so many fuses. So he stood up, expressed his thanks and showed the Lonsdale don to the door.

"There is just one thing," said Andrews. "I was meaning to mention it earlier, but you side-tracked me. Browne-Smith was never down to College breakfast in *my* time at Lonsdale—and that's fifteen years, now."

"Well, that's very interesting, sir," said Morse in a light tone that masked a heavy blow. "You've been extremely helpful, sir, and thank you for coming along. There's just one more thing. Please, if you will, convey my apologies to the College secretary. I'm sorry I was rude to her—I'd like her to know that."

"I'll certainly see that she does. She was upset, as I told you—and she's a lovely girl."

"Is she?" said Morse.

As soon as Andrews had gone, Morse reached for the phone to put his query to the curator of the Medical Science Library at the Bodleian, and, a few minutes later, he was listening carefully to the answer.

"It's the definitive work, inspector—Dr. J. P. F. Coole on *Carcinoma in the Brain*. This is what he's got to say—chapter six, by the way: 'Tumours are broadly divided into malignant tumours, which invade and destroy surrounding tissues; and benign tumours, which do not. Most malignant tumours have the additional property of giving rise to metastases or secondary tumours in parts of the body remote from the primary growth. A minority of malignant tumours fall into the category of tumours of local malignancy which invade and destroy surrounding tissues, but never metastasize. There are several tumours of local malignancy that occur in or on the head.'"

"Bit slower now," interposed Morse.

"'Many brain tumours are local in their malignancy; for example, the *spongioblastoma multiforme* and the diffuse *astrocytoma*. All tumours inside the skull are potentially fatal, even if they are quite benign—as this term has already been defined in—'"

"Thanks. That's fine. From what you're saying, then, it's possible that a brain-tumour might not spread to somewhere else in the body?"

"That's what this fellow says."

"Good. Now, one more thing. Would one of these brain-tumours perhaps result in some sort of irrationality? You know, doing things quite out of character?"

"Ah! That's in chapter seven. Just let me—"

"No, no. Just tell me vaguely, that'll be fine."

"Well, judging from the case-histories, the answer's a pretty definite 'yes.' *Very* strange things, some of them did."

"You see, I'm just wondering whether a man who'd got a brain-tumour, a man who'd been sober and meticulous all his life, might suddenly snap and—"

"By Jove, yes! Let me just quote that case of Olive Mainwearing from Manchester. Now, just let me—"

"No! Please don't bother. You've been wonderfully helpful, and I'm most grateful. The beer's on me next time we're together in the King's Arms."

Morse sat back in his black-leather chair, happily ignorant of the aforementioned Olive's extraordinary behaviour, and happily confident that at last he was beginning to see, through the mists, the outline of those further horizons.

CHAPTER
SIXTEEN

Thursday, 24th July

*Lewis again finds himself the unsuspecting cata-
lyst as Morse considers the course of the case so
far.*

When Lewis came in half an hour later, he found
Morse sitting motionless at his desk, staring down fixedly at
his blotting-pad, the orange-and-brown-striped scarf still
round his jaw, and the signature "On-no-account-disturb-
me" written overall.

Yet Lewis shattered the peace enthusiastically. "It was
Browne-Smith's typewriter, sir! Portable job, like you said.
No doubt about it."

Morse looked up slowly. "It was Westerby's typewriter—I thought I told you that."

"No, sir. It was *Browne-Smith's*. You must have made a
mistake. Believe me—you can't get two identical typewriters."

"I told you it was Westerby's," repeated Morse calmly.
"Perhaps you didn't hear me properly."

Lewis felt the anger rising within him: why couldn't
Morse—just for once!—allow a fraction of credit for what,
so conscientiously, he tried to do? "I *did* hear what you said.
You told me to find the typewriter—"

"I told you no such thing!" snapped Morse. "I told you
to get *Westerby's* typewriter. You *deaf?*"

Lewis breathed deeply, and very slowly shook his
head.

94

"Well? *Did* you get Westerby's typewriter?"

"It wasn't there," growled Lewis. "The removal people must have taken it. And don't blame me for that! As I just said, sir, it would do me good just once in a while to get a bit of thanks for—"

"Lew-is!" beamed Morse. "When—*when* will you begin to understand the value of virtually everything you do for me? Why do you misjudge me all the time? Listen! I remember perfectly well that the first sentence I typed out was done on Browne-Smith's typewriter, and the second on Westerby's. Now, just think! Since it was the *second*, as we know, that matched the letter we found in the dead man's pocket, it was on Westerby's typewriter that someone wrote our letter. Agreed? And now you come and tell me it was typed on Browne-Smith's? Well . . . you see what it all means, don't you?"

Over the years, Lewis had become skilled in situations such as this, knowing that Morse, like some inexperienced schoolmaster, was far more anxious to parade his own cleverness than to elicit any halting answer from his dimmer pupils. So it was that Lewis, with a knowing nod, sat back to listen.

"Of course you do! *Someone changed those typewriters*. And that, Lewis—does it not?—throws a completely new perspective on the whole case. And you know who's given me that new perspective? You!"

Sergeant Lewis sat back helplessly in his chair, feeling like a man just presented with the Wimbledon Challenge Cup after losing the last point of the tennis match. So he bowed towards the royal box, and waited. Not for long either, since Morse seemed excited.

"Tell me how you see this case, Lewis. You know—just in general."

"Well, I reckon Browne-Smith gets a letter from somebody who's terribly anxious to know how someone's got on in this examination, and he says if you'll scratch my back I'll scratch yours: just tell me that little bit early and I'll see you get your little reward."

"And then?"

"Well—like you, sir—this fellow Browne-Smith's a bachelor: he's quite tempted with the proposition put to him, and goes along with it."

"So?"

"Well, then he finds out that the people who run these sex-places in Soho are pretty hard boys."

"I wish you wouldn't start off every sentence with 'Well.'"

"You don't sound very convinced, sir?"

"Well, it all sounds a bit feeble, doesn't it? I mean, going to all that trouble just to get a girl's results a week or so early?"

"But you wouldn't understand these things. You've never had any children yourself, so you can't begin to imagine what it's like. I remember when my girls were expecting their eleven-plus results—then their O-Levels—waiting for the letter-box to rattle and then being scared to open the envelope; just hoping and praying there'd be some good news inside. It sort of gets you, sir—all that waiting. It's always at the back of your mind, and sometimes you'd give anything just to *know*. You realize *somebody* knows—somebody typing out the results and putting them into envelopes and all the rest of it. And I tell you one thing, sir: I'd have given a few quid myself to save me all that waiting and all that worriting."

Morse appeared temporarily touched by his sergeant's eloquence. "Look, Lewis. If that's all there is to it, why don't we just ring up this girl's father? You don't honestly think *he* wrote that letter, do you?"

"Jane Summers's dad, you mean?" Lewis shook his head. "Quite impossible, sir."

Morse sat upright in his chair. "Why do you say that?"

"Both her parents were killed in a car-crash six years ago—I rang up the college secretary. Very helpful, she was."

"Oh, I see." Morse unwound his scarf and looked a little lost. "Do you know, Lewis, I think you're a bit ahead of me in this case."

"No! I'm miles behind, sir—as well you know. But in my opinion we shouldn't rule out the parent angle altogether. She could only have been in her late teens when her parents died, and somebody must have had legal responsibility for her—an uncle or a guardian or something."

Morse's eyes were suddenly shining; and taking the torn letter from a drawer in his desk, he concentrated his brain upon it once more, his perusal punctuated by "Yes!", "Of course!", and finally "My son, you're a genius!"; whilst Lewis himself sank back in his chair and dropped back a further furlong in the case.

"Very illuminating," said Morse. "You say that not even the chairman would know the final results until a few hours before the lists are put up?"

Lewis nodded: "That's right."

"But doesn't that cock up just about everything?"

"Unless, sir," Lewis now felt happy with himself, "she was way out at the top of the list—the star of the whole show, sort of thing."

"Mm. We could ring up the chairman?"

"Which I have done, sir."

It was Morse himself who was happy now. The penicillin was working its wonders, and he felt strangely content. "And she *was* the top of the list, of course?"

Lewis, too, knew that life was sometimes very good. "She was, sir. And if you want my opinion—"

"Of course, I do!"

"—if this girl's uncle or whatever turns out to own a sex-club in Soho, we've probably found the key to the case, and the sooner we get up there the better."

"You've got a good point there, Lewis. On the other hand it's vital for one of us to stay here."

"Vital for *me*, I suppose?"

But Morse ignored the sarcasm, and adumbrated for the next half hour to his sergeant a few of the stranger thoughts that had criss-crossed his brain throughout the day.

It was getting late now; and, when Lewis left, Morse was free once more to indulge his own thoughts. At one time his mind would leap like a nimble-footed Himalayan goat; at another, it would stick for minutes on end like a leaden-footed diver in a sandbank. It was time to call it a day, that was obvious.

He was not quite finished, however, and before he left his office he did two things.

First, he amended his reconstruction of the fifth line of the torn letter so that it now read:

both you and me. My ward, Jane Summers of Lonsdale

Second, he took a sheet of paper and wrote the following short piece (reproduced below as it appeared in the *Oxford Mail* the following day):

CLUE TO MURDER

Customers of Marks and Spencers in the Oxford area are being asked to join in the hunt for the murderer of a 60-year-old man found in the canal at Thrupp. The bloodstained socks on the body (not yet identified) have been traced as one of just 2,500 pairs distributed around a handful of M & S stores in the Oxford region. The socks were of navy-blue cotton, with two light blue rings round the tops. Anyone who might have any information is asked to ring Kidlington 4343.

Only after dictating this absurd news-item (comma included) did Morse finally leave his office that day to return to his bachelor flat. There he played through the first act of *Die Walküre* and began to make significant inroads into the bottle just purchased from Augustus Barnett. When, at midnight, he looked around for his pyjamas, he couldn't quite remember why he had bothered the newspaper editor; yet he knew that when a man was utterly at a loss about what he should do, it was imperative that he should do *something*—like the motorist stuck in a snowdrift who decided to activate his blinkers alternately.

CHAPTER
SEVENTEEN

Friday, 25th July

*Discussion of identity, and of death, leads the two
detectives gradually nearer to the truth.*

Lewis came in early the next morning (although not so
early as Morse), and immediately got down to reading the
medical report from the lab.

"Gruesome all this, isn't it, sir?"

"Not read it," replied Morse.

"You know, chopping a chap's head off."

"It's one way of killing someone. After all, the experi-
ment has been tried on innumerable occasions and found to
be invariably fatal."

"But the head was cut off *after* he was dead—says so
here."

"I don't give two monkeys *how* he was killed. It's the
why that we've got to sort out. *Why* did someone chop his
head off—just tell me that, for a start."

"Because we'd have identified him, surely. His teeth
would have been there and—"

"Come off it! Helluva job that'd be, hawking some den-
tal chart round a few million dentists—"

"Thousands, you mean."

"—and perhaps he didn't *have* any teeth, like sometimes I wish I hadn't."

"It says here that this chap might have been killed
somewhere else and taken out to the canal later."

"So?"

99

"What do people usually get carried around in?" asked Lewis.

"Cars?" (Morse hardly enjoyed being catechized himself.)

"Exactly! So if the body was too big to get into the boot of the car. . . ."

"You cut him down to size."

"That's it. It's like one of those ghost things, sir. You sort of tuck the head underneath the arm."

"Where's the head now, then?"

"Somewhere in the canal."

"The frogmen haven't found it."

"Heads are pretty heavy, though. It's probably stuck way down in the mud."

"What about the *hands,* Lewis? You reckon we're going to find them neatly folded next to the head? Or is some poor little beggar going to find them in his fishing-net?"

"You don't seem to think we're going to find them, sir."

Morse was showing signs of semi-exasperation. "You're missing the bloody point, Lewis! I'm not asking *where* they are. I'm asking *why* someone chopped them off."

"Same as before. Must be because someone could have identified them. He may have had a tattoo on the back of his wrist or something."

Morse sat quite still. He knew even then that Lewis had made a point of quite extraordinary significance, and his mind, like some downhill skier, had suddenly leaped into the air across a ridge and landed neatly upon a track of virgin snow. . . .

Lewis's voice seemed to reach his ears as if through a wadge of tightly-packed cotton wool. "And what about the legs, sir. Why do you think *they* were chopped off?"

"You mean *you* know?" Morse heard himself saying.

"Hardly that, sir. But it's child's play these days for the forensic boys to find a hundred-and-one things on clothes, isn't it? Hairs and threads and all that sort of thing—"

"Even if it's been in water for a few days?"

"Well, it might be more difficult then, I agree. But all I'm saying is that if we knew whose the body was—"

"We do, Lewis. You can be sure of that—surer than ever. It's Browne-Smith's."

"All right. If it's Browne-Smith's body, then we shan't have much trouble in finding out if it's Browne-Smith's *suit*, shall we?"

Morse was frowning in genuine puzzlement. "You're losing me, Lewis."

"All I'm trying to say, sir, is that if someone carefully chopped off this fellow's head and his hands to stop us finding out who he was—"

"Yes?"

"—well, I don't reckon he would have left the fellow dressed in his own suit."

"So someone dressed the corpse in someone else's suit, is that it?"

"Yes. You see, a lot of people could wear each other's jackets. I mean, I could wear yours—you're a bit fatter than I am round the middle, but it'd fit in a way. And with a jacket in the water a few days, it'd probably shrink a bit anyway, so no one's going to notice too much. *But*—" and here Lewis paused dramatically "—if people start wearing each other's trousers, sir—well, you could find a few problems, couldn't you? They might be too long, or too short; and it wouldn't be difficult for anyone to see almost immediately that the suit was someone else's. Do you see what I mean? I think the dead man must have been several inches shorter, or several inches taller, than the fellow whose suit he was dressed in! And *that's* why the legs were chopped off. So as I see it, sir, if we can find out whose suit it is, we shall know one thing for certain: the owner of the suit isn't the corpse—he's probably the murderer!"

Morse sat where he was, looking duly impressed and appreciative. As a result of his visit to the dentist he had himself arrived at a very similar conclusion (although by a completely different route), but he felt it proper to congratulate his sergeant.

"You know, they say your eyes begin to deteriorate about the age of seven or eight, and that your brain follows suit about twenty years later. But your brain, Lewis. It seems to get sharper every day."

Lewis leaned back happily. "Must be working with you, sir."

But Morse appeared not to hear him, staring out (as Lewis had so often seen him) across the concreted yard that lay outside his window. And thus he stared for many, many minutes; and Lewis had almost read the medical report through a second time before Morse spoke again.

"It's very sad about life, really, you know. There's only one thing certain about it, and that's death. We all die, sooner or later. Even old Max, with all his laudable caution, would probably accept that. 'The boast of heraldry, the pomp of power. . . .'"

"Pardon, sir?"

"We shall all die, Lewis—even you and me—just like that poor fellow we fished out of the pond. There are no exceptions."

"Wasn't there just the *one*?" asked Lewis, quietly.

"You believe that?"

"Yes."

"Mm."

"Why do you mention all this, sir—you know, about dying and so on?"

"I was just thinking about Browne-Smith, that's all. I was just thinking that a man we all thought was dead is probably alive again—that's all."

That's all. For a little while Lewis had almost convinced himself that he might be a move or two ahead of Morse. Yet now, as he shook his head in customary bewilderment, he knew that Morse's mind was half a dozen moves ahead of all the world. So he sat where he was, like a disciple in the Scriptures at the feet of the Master, wondering why he ever bothered to think about anything himself at all.

CHAPTER
EIGHTEEN

Friday, 25th July

Morse decides to enjoy the hospitality of yet another member of Lonsdale's top brass, whilst Lewis devotes himself to the donkey work.

It was high time something was done, Morse knew that. There was the dead man's suit to start with, for surely Lewis had been right in maintaining that the minutest detritus of living would still be lingering somewhere in the most improbable crannies of pockets and sleeves. Then there was the mysterious man Gilbert, who had been given free (and official) access to the room in which the two letters had probably been typed: Gilbert the furniture-man, who might at that very minute be shifting the last of the crates and the crockery . . . Yes, it was high time the pair of them actually *did* something. *Necesse erat digitos extrahere*.

Morse was (as almost always when in a car) a morose and uncommunicative passenger as Lewis drove down to Lonsdale via St. Giles's and the Cornmarket, then left at Carfax and into The High. At the Lodge, it was the same young porter on duty. But this time he refused to hand over the keys to any room before consulting higher authority; and Morse was still trying to get through to the Bursar when a man walked into the Lodge whom he had seen several times when he had dined at Lonsdale. It was the Vice-Master.

Ten minutes later, Lewis, with two keys in his hand,

was climbing up the steps of Staircase T, whilst Morse was seating himself comfortably in a deep armchair in the Vice-Master's suite, and agreeing that although it was rather early in the day a glass of something might not be totally unwelcome.

"So you see, inspector" (it was several minutes later) "it's not a very happy story at all—not an unusual one, though. That pair could never have got on together, whatever happened; but there were no signs of open animosity—not, as I say, until five years ago."

"Since when they've never even spoken to each other?"

"That's it."

"And the reason for all this?"

"Oh, there's no great secret about that. I should think almost everyone in the college knows, apart from one or two of the younger fellows."

"Tell me about it."

It appeared that only two crucial ordinances had been decreed for election to the Mastership of Lonsdale College: first, that any nominand must be a layman; second, that such a person must be elected by the eight senior fellows of the college, with a minimum of six votes needed in favour, and with the election declared invalid if even a single vote was cast against. It had been common knowledge five years ago, in spite of the so-called "secret" nature of the ballot, that when Dr. Browne-Smith had been proposed and seconded, one solitary vote had thwarted his election hopes; equally common knowledge was the fact that when Mr. Westerby's name, in turn, had been put forward, one single slip of paper was firmly printed with a "No." The third choice—the compromise candidate—had also been one of the college's senior fellows, and it had been a relief for everyone when the present Master had been voted into office, *nem. con.*

"Head of House!" said Morse slowly. "Great honour, isn't it?" (He was suddenly conscious that he had repeated *verbatim* the question he had asked of Andrews.)

"Some people would give a lot for it, yes."

"Would *you*?"

The Vice-Master smiled. "No! You can leave me out of the running, inspector. You see, I'm in holy orders, and so, as I said, I'm just not eligible."

"I see," said Morse. "Now just getting back to Dr. Browne-Smith for a minute. I'd be grateful, sir, if you could tell me something about his, well, his personal life."

"Such as?" The Vice-Master's eyes were upon him, and Morse found himself wondering how much, or how little, he could ever expect to know of the complex web of relationships within this tight community of Lonsdale.

"What about his health, for example?"

Again the shrewd look, as if the question had been fully expected. "He was a very sick man, inspector. But you knew that yesterday, didn't you? By the way, Andrews said you looked just a little surprised when he told you."

"How long had *you* known?" countered Morse.

"Three weeks, I suppose. The Master called Andrews and me up to his room one evening after Hall. Strictly confidential, he said, and all that—but we had to know, of course, because of Browne-Smith's teaching commitments."

"When did the Master think. . . ?"

"Certainly no longer than the end of the Hilary Term."

"Mm."

"And you're wondering whether his teaching days might not be over already. Am I right?"

"How much did Andrews tell you?" asked Morse.

"Everything. You didn't mind, I hope?"

Morse felt oddly uncomfortable with the man, and after asking a few more vague questions about Browne-Smith's lifestyle, he got up to go. "You getting some holiday soon, sir?"

"Once the Master gets back. We usually alternate so that one of us is here for most of the vac. I know that some people haven't much time for all us lazy academic lay-abouts, but there's a lot to do in a college apart from looking after students. But you'd know that, of course."

Morse nodded, and knew that he could very soon learn to dislike this unclerically-garbed parson intensely.

"We shall co-operate as much as we can," continued the Vice-Master. "You know that. But it would be nice to be kept in the picture—just a little, perhaps?"

"Nothing really to tell you, sir—not yet, anyway."

"You don't even want to tell me why your sergeant took the key to Westerby's room as well?"

"Ah, that! Yes, I ought to have mentioned that, sir. You see, there's just a possibility that the corpse we found up in the canal wasn't Browne-Smith's after all."

"Really?"

But Morse declined to elaborate further as he made his farewell and strode away across the quad, sensing those highly intelligent eyes upon him as he turned into the Porters' Lodge. From there he progressed, only some hundred yards, into the bar of the Mitre, where he had agreed to meet Lewis. He would be half an hour early, he realized that; but a thirty-minute wait in a pub was no great trial of patience to Morse.

Once inside Browne-Smith's room, Lewis had taken out of its plastic wrapper the dark-blue jacket found on the corpse and measured it carefully against the jackets in the bedroom wardrobe: it was the same length, the same measurement round the chest, of the same sartorial style, with a single slit at the back and slim lapels. There could be little doubt about it: the jacket had belonged to Browne-Smith. After rehanging the suits, Lewis methodically looked through the rest of the clothes, but learned only that each of the five pairs of shoes was size nine, and that four brand-new pairs of socks were all of navy-blue cotton with two light blue rings round the tops.

Westerby's rooms opposite were silent and empty now, only the faded-brown fitted carpet remaining, with oblong patches of pristine colour marking the erstwhile positions of the heavier furniture. Nothing else at all, except a plastic spoon and an empty jar of Nescafé on the draining-board in the kitchen.

Lewis's highly discreet enquiries in the college office produced (amongst other things) the information that Browne-Smith certainly wore a suit very similar to the one he now unwrapped once more; and the college secretary herself (whom even Lewis considered very beautiful) was firmest of all in such sad corroboration.

The young porter was still on duty when Lewis handed back the two keys, and was soon chatting freely enough when Lewis asked about "Gilbert Removals." As far as the porter could remember, Mr. Gilbert himself had been down to T Staircase about four or five times; but he'd finished now, for Mr. Westerby had at last been "shifted."

"Funny you should ask about Mr. Gilbert, sergeant. He's like your chief—both of 'em got the jaw-ache by the look of things."

Lewis nodded and prepared to leave. "Nuisance, teeth are, yes. Nothing much worse than an abscess on one of your front teeth, you know."

The porter looked strangely at Lewis for a few seconds, for the words he had just heard were almost exactly (he could swear it) the words he had heard from the afflicted furniture-remover.

He told Lewis so . . . and Lewis told Morse, in the Mitre. Yet neither of them realized, at least for the present, that this brief and seemingly insignificant little episode was to have a profound effect upon the later stages of the case.

CHAPTER NINETEEN

Friday, 25th July

*Our two detectives have not yet quite finished
with the implications of severe dismemberment.*

The case was working out well enough, thought Lewis,
as he drove Morse back through Summertown. The shops
were in the same order as they'd been two hours earlier
when he had driven past them: the RAC building, Budg-
ens, Straw Hat Bakery, Allied Carpets, Chicken Barbecue
. . . yes, just the same. It was only a question of seeing
them in reverse order now, tracing them backwards, as it
were. Just like this case. Morse had traced things backwards fairly well thus far, if somewhat haphazardly. . . .
And he wanted to ask Morse two questions, though he
knew better than to interrupt the great man's thoughts in
transit.

In Morse's mind, too, far more was surfacing from the
murky waters of a local canal than a bloated, mutilated
corpse that had been dragged in by a boat-hook as it threatened to drift down again and out of reach. Other things had
been surfacing all the way along the towpath, as clue had
followed clue. One thing at least was fairly firmly estab-
lished: the murderer—whoever that might be—had either
been quite extraordinarily subtle, or quite inordinately stu-
pid, in going to the lengths of dismembering a body, and
then leaving it in its own clothes. If it *was* in its own suit
. . . Lewis had done his job; and Lewis was sure that the
suit was Browne-Smith's. But what about the body? Oh yes,
indeed—but what about the body?

Back in Morse's office, Lewis launched into his questions: "It's pretty certainly Browne-Smith's body, don't you think, sir?"

"Don't know."

"But surely—"

"I said I don't *bloody* know!"

So, Lewis, after a decent interval, asked his other question: "Don't you think it's a bit of a coincidence that you and this Gilbert fellow should have a bad tooth at the same time?"

Morse appeared to find this an infinitely more interesting question, and he made no immediate reply. Then he shook his head decisively. "No. Coincidences are far more commonplace than any of us are willing to accept. It's this whole business of *chance*, Lewis. We don't go in much for talking about chance and luck, and what a huge part they play in all our lives. But the Greeks did—*and* the Romans; they both used to worship the goddess of luck. And if you must go on about coincidences, you just go home tonight and find the forty-sixth word from the beginning of the forty-sixth psalm, and the forty-sixth word from the end of it—and see what you land up with! Authorized Version, by the way."

"Say that again, sir?"

"Forget it, Lewis! Now, listen! Let's just get back to this case we're landed with and what we were talking about at lunchtime. If our murderer wants his victim to be identified, he does not—repeat *not* chop his head off. Quite apart from the facial features—features that could be recognized by some myopic moron from thirty yards away—you've got your balding head, your missing mandibles, and whatever—even the angle of your ears; and all of those things are going to lead to a certain identification. Somebody's going to know who he is, whether he's been floating in the Mississippi for a fortnight, or whether he's been up in Thrupp for three months. Agreed? And if our murderer is still anxious for his corpse to be identified, he does not—repeat *not* cut his hands off, either. Because that removes at one fell chop the one thing we know that gives him a unique and unquestionable individuality—his fingerprints!"

"What about the legs, sir?"

"Shut up a minute! And for Christ's sake try to follow what I'm telling you! It's hard enough for *me*!"

"I'm not finding much trouble, sir."

"All I'm saying is that if the murderer wants the body to be recognized, he doesn't chop off his head and he doesn't chop off his hands—agreed?"

Lewis nodded: he agreed.

"And yet, Lewis, there are two other clues that lead quite clearly to a positive identification of the body; the suit—quite certainly now it seems it was Browne-Smith's suit; and then the letter—almost as certainly that was written to Browne-Smith. All right, it wasn't all *that* obvious; but you'd hardly need to be a Shylock—"

"'Sherlock,' sir."

"You see what I'm getting at, though?"

Lewis pondered the question, and finally answered, "No."

Morse, too, was beginning to wonder whether he himself was following the drift of his own logic, but he'd always had the greatest faith in the policy of mouthing the most improbable notions, in the sure certainty that by the law of averages some of them stood a more reasonable chance of being nearer to the truth than others. So he burbled on.

"Just suppose for a minute, Lewis, that the body *isn't* Browne-Smith's, but that somebody wanted it to *look* like his. All right? Now, if the murderer had left us the head, or the hands, or both, then we could have been quite sure that the body *wasn't* Browne-Smith's, couldn't we? As we know, Browne-Smith was suffering from an incurable brain-tumour, and with a skull stuck on the table in front of him even old Max might have been able to tell us there was something not all that healthy round the cerebral cortex— even if the facial features were badly disfigured. It's just the same with the hands—quite apart from fingerprints. Browne-Smith lost most of his right index-finger in the war, and not even your micro-surgeons can stick an artificial digit on your hand without even a delinquent like Dickson spotting it. So, if the hands, or at least the right hand, had been left attached to the body, and *if all the fingers were intact—*

then again we'd have been quite sure that the body *wasn't* Browne-Smith's. You follow me? The two things that could have proved that the body wasn't his are both deliberately and callously removed."

Lewis frowned, just about managing to follow the line of Morse's argument. "But what about the suit? What about the letter?"

"All I'm saying, Lewis, is that perhaps someone's been trying mighty hard to convince us that it *was* Browne-Smith's body, that's all."

"Aren't you making it all a bit too complicated?"

"Could be," conceded Morse.

"I'm just a bit lost, you see, sir. We're usually looking for a murderer, aren't we? We've never had all this trouble with a body before."

Morse nodded. "But we're getting to know more about the murderer all the time! He's a very clever chap. He tries to lead us astray about the identity of the body, and he very nearly succeeds."

"So?"

"So he's almost as clever as we are; and most of the clever people I know are—guess where, Lewis!"

"In the police force?"

Morse allowed himself a weak smile, but continued with his previous earnestness. "In the University of Oxford! And what's more, I reckon I've got a jolly good idea about exactly *which* member of the University it is!"

"Uh?" Lewis looked across at his chief with surprise—and suspicion.

But Morse was off again. "Let's just finish off this corpse. We're left with those legs, right? Now we've got some ideas about the head and the hands, but why chop the legs off?"

"Perhaps he lost a toe in a swimming accident off Bermuda or somewhere. Got his foot caught in the propeller of a boat or something."

Morse was suddenly very still in his chair, for Lewis's flippant answer had lit another sputtering fuse. He reached for the phone, rang through on an internal extension to Superintendent Strange, and (to Lewis's complete surprise) asked for two more frogmen—if possible immediately—to search the bottom of the canal by Aubrey's Bridge.

"Now about those legs," resumed Morse. "At what point would you say they were chopped off?"

"Well, sort of here, sir." Lewis vaguely put his hand on his femur. "About halfway between—"

"Between pelvis and patella, that's right. Halfway, though, you say? But if we don't know how long his thighs were to start with, where exactly is that 'halfway' of yours? It may have been meant to *look* halfway—"

"That's what I told you this morning, sir."

"I know you did, yes! All I'm doing is to stick a bit more clarity into your thinking. You don't mind, I hope?"

"My mind's perfectly clear already, sir. He might have been a shorter man or a taller man, and, because Browne-Smith's about five-eleven, the odds are probably on him being shorter. It's the length of the femur, you see, that largely determines the height."

"Oh!" said Morse. "You don't happen to know how tall Westerby is—or was?"

"Five-five, sir—about that. I asked the college secretary—very nice girl."

"Oh!"

"And I agree with all you've said, sir. Head, hands, legs—you've explained them all. If the murderer wanted us to think the body was Browne-Smith's, perhaps he couldn't have left any of them."

The tables were turned now, and it was Morse's turn to look dubious. "You don't think all this is getting a bit too complicated, do you, Lewis?"

"*Far* too complicated. We've got the suit and we've got the letter—both of them Browne-Smith's—and we know that he's gone missing somewhere. That would be quite enough for me, sir. But you seem to think that the man we're after is almost as clever as you are."

Morse did not reply immediately, and Lewis noticed the look of curious exhilaration in the Chief Inspector's face. What, he wondered, had he suddenly thought of now?

Dickson called in a few minutes later to report that no one by the name of Simon Rowbotham was registered in the membership of the Pike Anglers' Association or in the membership of any other fishing-club in the vicinity of Oxford; and Lewis was disappointed with this news, for it gave a little more weight to the one freakish objection to his own firm view that the corpse they had found must be Browne-Smith's: the objection (as Morse had pointed out to him the previous morning) that *"Simon Rowbotham" was an exact anagram of "O.M.A. Browne-Smith."*

CHAPTER TWENTY

Saturday, 26th July

An extremely brief envoi to the first part of the case.

At five minutes to four the next morning, Morse awoke and looked at his bedside clock. It seemed quite impossible that it should be so early, for he felt completely refreshed. He got out of bed and drew the curtains, standing for several minutes looking down on the utterly silent road, only a hundred yards from Banbury Road roundabout . . . the road that led north out to Kidlington, and thence past the Thames Valley Police HQ up to the turn for Thrupp, where the waters would now be lapping and plopping gently against the houseboats as they lay at their overnight moorings.

Morse went into the bathroom, noticed that his jaw was almost normal again, swallowed the last of the penicillin tablets and returned to bed, where he lay on his back, his hands behind his head. . . . There were still many pieces of flotsam that needed to be salvaged before the wreck of a man's life could wholly be reconstructed . . . salvaged from those canal waters which changed their colour from green to grey to yellow to black . . . to white. . . . Morse almost dozed off again, momentarily imagining that he saw the outlines of a cunningly plotted murder, with himself—yes, Morse!—at the centre of a beautifully calculated deception. Of one thing he was now utterly sure: that, quite contrary to Lewis's happy convictions about the identity of the dead

114

man, *the man they had found was quite certainly not Dr. Browne-Smith of Lonsdale*.

Thereafter, Morse was impatient for the morning and for traffic noise and for the sight of people catching buses. Ovid, in the arms of his lover, and cried out to the midnight horses to gallop slow across the vault of heaven. But Morse was without a lover; and at a quarter to five he got up, made himself a cup of tea and looked out once again at the quiet street below, where he sensed a few vague flutterings and stirrings from the chrysalis of night.

And Morse sensed rightly. For the next morning, like Browne-Smith before him, he received a long letter; a strange and extremely exciting letter.

THE END OF THE FIRST MILE

THE
SECOND
MILE

CHAPTER
TWENTY-ONE

Monday, 28th July

*Morse, having been put on the right track by the
wrong clues, now finds his judgement almost
wholly vindicated.*

Morse opened the door of his office a few minutes after
eight to find Lewis reading the *Daily Mirror*.

"You seem very anxious to further our enquiries this
morning, Lewis."

Lewis folded up the newspaper. "I'm afraid you've
made a bad mistake, sir."

"You mean you *are* busy on the case?"

"Not only that, sir. As I say, you've made a bad mistake."

"Nonsense!"

"I was trying to do the coffee-break crossword and
there was a clue there that just said 'Carthorse (anagram)'—"

"'Orchestra,'" interrupted Morse.

"I know that, sir. But 'Simon Rowbotham' is *not* an anagram of 'O.M.A. Browne-Smith'!"

"Of course it is!" Morse immediately wrote down the
letters, and was checking them off one by one when suddenly he stopped. "My God! You're right. There's an 'o' instead of an 'e,' isn't there?"

"It was only by chance I checked it when I was—"

But Morse wasn't listening. Was he *wrong*, after all his
mighty thoughts and bold deductions? Was Lewis *right*—
with his simple-minded assertion that the case was becom-

ing quite unnecessarily complicated? He shook his head in some dismay. Perhaps (he clutched at straws), perhaps if he himself had made a mistake over an anagram, so might Browne-Smith have done in concocting a completely bogus name? But he couldn't convince even himself for a second, and the truth was that he felt lost.

At eight-thirty the phone rang, an excited voice announcing itself as Constable Dickson.

"I've just been reading last week's *Oxford Times*, sir."

"Not on duty, I hope."

"I'm off duty, sir. I'm at home."

"Oh."

"I've found him!"

"Found who?"

"Simon Rowbotham. I was reading the angling page—and his name's there. He came second in a fishing match out at King's Weir last Sunday."

"Oh."

"He lives in Botley, so it says."

"I don't give a sod if he lives in Bootle."

"Pardon, sir?"

"Thanks for letting me know, anyway."

"Remember what you said about those doughnuts, sir?"

"No, I forget," said Morse, and put the receiver down.

"Shall I go out and see him?" asked Lewis quietly.

"What the hell good would that do?" snapped Morse, thereafter lapsing into sullen silence.

Since it was marked "Strictly Private and Confidential," the Registry had not opened the bulky white envelope, and it was lying there on Morse's blue blotting-pad when later the two men returned from coffee. Inside the envelope was a further sealed envelope (addressed, like the outer cover, to Chief Inspector E. Morse), and a covering letter from the Manager of the High Street branch of Barclays Bank, dated 26th July. It read as follows:

Dear Sir,

We received the sealed envelope enclosed on Monday, 21st July, with instructions that it be posted to you personally on Saturday, 26th July. We trust you agree that we have discharged our obligation.

Yours faithfully . . .

Morse handed the note over to Lewis. "What do you make of that?"

"Seems a lot of palaver to me, sir. Why not just post it straight to you?"

"I dunno," said Morse. "Let's hope it's full of fivers."

"Aren't you going to open it?"

"Interesting," said Morse, apparently unhearing. "If this letter reached the bank on Monday, the 21st, it was probably written on Sunday, the 20th—and Max says that's the likeliest day that someone put the corpse in the canal."

"But it's probably nothing to do with the case."

"Well, we'll soon know." Morse slit the envelope and began reading, and apart from a solitary "My God!" (after the first few lines of the typewritten script) he read in utter silence, as totally engrossed, it seemed, as a dedicated pornophilist in a sex-shop.

When he had finished the long letter, he wore that look of almost sickening self-satisfaction frequently found on the face of any man whose judgement had been called into question, but thereafter proved correct.

Lewis took the letter now, immediately turning to the last page. "There's no signature, sir."

"Read it—just read it, Lewis," said Morse blandly, as he reached for the phone and dialed the number of the bank.

"Manager, please."

"He's rather tied up at the minute. Could you—"

"Chief Constable of Oxfordshire here, lad. Just tell him to get to the phone, please." (Lewis had by now read the first page of the letter.)

"Can I help you?" asked the manager.

"I want to know whether Dr. Browne-Smith—Dr. O. M. A. Browne-Smith—of Lonsdale College is one of your clients."

"Yes, he is."

"We received a letter from you today, sir, and it's my duty to ask you if it was Dr. Browne-Smith himself who asked you to forward it to us."

"Ah, the letter, yes. I hoped the Post Office wouldn't keep you waiting too long."

"You haven't answered my question, sir."

"No, I haven't. And I can't, I'm afraid."

"I think you can, sir, and I think you will—because we're caught up in a case of murder."

"Murder? You're not—you're not saying Browne-Smith's been murdered, surely?"

"No, I didn't say that."

"Could you tell me exactly who it is that's been murdered?"

Morse hesitated—for too long. "No, I can't, not just for the present. Enquiries are still at a very—er—delicate stage, and that's why we've got to expect the co-operation of everyone concerned—people like yourself, sir."

The manager was also hesitant. "It's very difficult for me. You see, it involves the whole question of the confidentiality of the bank."

Morse sounded surprisingly mild and accommodating. "I understand, sir. Let's leave it, shall we, for the present? But if it becomes an absolutely vital piece of information, we shall naturally have to come and question you."

"Yes, I see that. But I shall have to take the matter up with the bank's legal advisers, of course."

"Very sensible, sir. And thank you for your co-operation."

Lewis, who had been half-reading the letter (with continued amazement) and also half-listening to this strange telephone conversation, now looked up to see Morse smiling serenely and waiting patiently for him to finish.

When he had done so, but before he had the chance to pass any comment, Morse asked him to give Barclays an-

Introducing the first and only complete hardcover collection of Agatha Christie's mysteries

Now you can enjoy the
greatest mysteries ever written
in a magnificent
Home Library Edition.

Discover Agatha Christie's world of mystery, adventure and intrigue

Agatha Christie's timeless tales of mystery and suspense offer something for every reader—mystery fan or not—young and old alike. And now, you can build a complete hardcover library of her world-famous mysteries by subscribing to The Agatha Christie Mystery Collection.

This exciting Collection is your passport to a world where mystery reigns supreme. Volume after volume, you and your family will enjoy mystery reading at its very best.

You'll meet Agatha Christie's world-famous detectives like Hercule Poirot, Jane Marple, and the likeable Tommy and Tuppence Beresford.

In your readings, you'll visit Egypt, Paris, England and other exciting destinations where murder is always on the itinerary. And wherever you travel, you'll become deeply involved in some of the most ingenious and diabolical plots ever invented ... "cliff-hangers" that only Dame Agatha could create!

It all adds up to mystery reading that's so good ... it's almost criminal. And it's yours every month with The Agatha Christie Mystery Collection.

Solve the greatest mysteries of all time. The Collection contains all of Agatha Christie's classic works including *Murder on the Orient Express, Death on the Nile, And Then There Were None, The ABC Murders* and her ever-popular whodunit, *The Murder of Roger Ackroyd.*

Each handsome hardcover volume is Smythe sewn and printed on high quality acid-free paper so it can withstand even the most murderous treatment. Bound in Sussex-blue simulated leather with gold titling, The Agatha Christie Mystery Collection will make a tasteful addition to your living room, or den.

Ride the Orient Express for 10 days without obligation.
To introduce you to the Collection, we're inviting you to examine the classic mystery, *Murder on the Orient Express*, without risk or obligation. If you're not completely satisfied, just return it within 10 days and owe nothing.

However, if you're like the millions of other readers who love Agatha Christie's thrilling tales of mystery and suspense, keep *Murder on the Orient Express* and pay just $9.95 plus postage and handling.

You will then automatically receive future volumes once a month as they are published on a fully returnable, 10-day free-examination basis. No minimum purchase is required, and you may cancel your subscription at any time.

This unique collection is not sold in stores. It's available only through this special offer. So don't miss out, begin your subscription now. Just mail this card today.

☐ Yes! Please send me *Murder on the Orient Express* for a 10-day free-examination and enter my subscription to <u>The Agatha Christie Mystery Collection</u>. If I keep *Murder on the Orient Express*, I will pay just $9.95 plus postage and handling and receive one additional volume each month on a fully returnable 10-day free-examination basis. There is no minimum number of volumes to buy, and I may cancel my subscription at any time.   70110

Name_____

Address_____

City_____ State_____ Zip_____

QB

**Send No Money...
But Act Today!**

BUSINESS REPLY MAIL

FIRST CLASS   PERMIT NO. 2154   HICKSVILLE, N.Y.

Postage will be paid by addressee:

The Agatha Christie
Mystery Collection
Bantam Books
P.O. Box 956
Hicksville, N.Y. 11802

other ring, to tell them he was Chief Inspector Morse, and to find out whether they had a second client on their books: a Mr. George Westerby, of Lonsdale.

The answer was quick and unequivocal: yes, they had.

CHAPTER
TWENTY-TWO

We have an exact transcript of the long letter,
which was without salutation or subscription,
studied by Chief Inspector Morse and by Ser-
geant Lewis, in the mid-morning of Monday, 28th
July.

"Perhaps it is not too much to expect that you have
made the necessary investigations? It would scarcely need
an intellect as (potentially) powerful as your own accurately
to have traced the sequence of events thus far. After all, you
had my suit, did you not? That, most surely, should have led
your assistants to my (agreed, rather limited) wardrobe at
Lonsdale, where (I assume) the waist-band inches and the
inside-leg measurements have already been minutely
matched. But let us agree: the body was not mine. I did try,
perhaps amateurishly, to make you think it was; yet I had
little doubt that you would quickly piece together a reasonably coherent letter, the torn half of which I left in the back
pocket of the trousers. You might therefore have had the
reasonable suspicion that the corpse was me—but not for
long, if I assess you right.

"But whichever way it is (either your thinking of me as
one of the dead or as one of the non-dead), I see it my duty
to inform you that I am alive, at least for a little while
longer. (You will have discovered that, too?) Whose, then, is
the body you found in the waters out at Thrupp? For it is
not, most certainly not, my own. I repeat—whose is it? To
find the answer to that question must be your next task, and
it is a task in which I am prepared (even anxious) to offer

some co-operation. As a child, did you ever play the game called 'treasure-hunt,' wherein a clue would lead from A to B? From, let us say, a little message hidden underneath a stone to a further message pinned behind a maple-tree? Well, let us go on a little, shall we? From B to C, as it were.

"I received the letter and immediately acted upon it. All very odd, was it not? I knew the girl mentioned, of course, for she was one of my own pupils; and, what is more, she was a girl acknowledged by all to be the outstanding classic of the year—if not of the decade. This was common knowledge, and it was totally predictable (why bother to ask me?) that her marks in the Greats papers would be higher than any of her contemporaries of either sex. Therefore the request to communicate (and that to some anonymous third party) this particular girl's result only a week or so before the publication of class-lists struck me as rather suspicious. (A poorly constructed sentence, but I have not time to recast it.) My reward, I was told, for divulging the result some days early would be a memorably pleasant one. You would agree, I think? Even an ageing (I always put the 'e' in that word) bachelor like myself may be permitted his mildly erotic day-dreams. And, as I believe, I would hardly be committing the ultimate sin in informing the world of what the world already knew. But I am not telling you the whole truth, even now. Let me go back a little.

"I have a colleague living directly opposite me: a Mr. G. Westerby. He and I have been fellow dons for far too many years, and it is an open secret that the relations between the two of us have been almost childishly hostile for a great deal of that time. This colleague (I prefer not to mention his name again) is now retiring; and, although I have never actively sought to learn of his immediate plans, I have naturally gleaned a few desultory facts about his purposes: he is now away on one of his customary cut-price holidays in the Greek islands; he is, on his return, to take up residence in some pretentiously fashionable flat in the Bloomsbury district; he has recently hired a firm of removal people to pack up the cheap collection of bric-à-brac his philistine tastes have considered valuable enough to accumulate during his overlong stay in the University. (Please forgive my cynical words.)

"Now—please pay careful attention! One day, only a few weeks ago, I saw a man walking up my own staircase; the man did not see me—not at that point, anyway. He looked around him, at first with the diffidence of a stranger, then with the confidence of an intimate; and he took the key he was holding and inserted it into Westerby's oak. For myself, I took little notice. If someone wished to burgle my colleague's valueless belongings, I felt little inclination to interfere. In fact, I was secretly interested—and amused. I learned that this stranger was the head of a London removals firm; that he had come to size up the task and to pack up the goods. A few days later, I saw this same individual again—although this time he wore a bright red scarf about his face, as if the wind blew uncommonly keenly, or as if the wretched fellow had recently returned from the dentist's chair. It was only a matter of days after this that I received a letter—<u>istam epistolam</u>; the letter you half-received yourself.

"Does all this sound rather mysterious and puzzling? No! Not to you, surely. For you have already guessed what I am about to say. Yes! I recognized the man; and the man brought back poignantly to me the one episode in my life of which I am bitterly—so bitterly!—ashamed. But again, I am getting ahead of myself—or behind. It depends upon which way you look at it.

"With assorted young assistants, this man reappeared three or four times, presumably to supervise the packing-up of crates and boxes in my colleague's rooms. And on each of these subsequent occasions, the man wore the same gaudy scarf around the lower half of his face, as if (as I have said) a wayward tooth was inflicting upon him the acutest agony . . . or else as if he wished to keep his face concealed. Is one not, in such circumstances, quite justified in adding two and two together, and making of them twenty-two? Was he worried, perhaps, that I should recognize his face? Had he known it, however, his clumsy attempts at deception were futile. Why? Simply because <u>I had already recognized the man.</u> And because of this, I experienced little difficulty in linking the two contiguous events together: first, the arrival in Lonsdale of the one man in the world I had hoped and prayed I would never meet again; second, the arrival of the strangest letter I ever received in the whole of my time in the college. In sum, these two events appeared to me to add to more than twenty-two; yet not to more than I could cope with. Let us go on a bit.

"I followed up my invitation. Why not do so? I have never married. I have never, therefore, known the delights (if such they are) of the marriage-bed. Over-rated as I have frequently considered them, the illicit lure of sexual delights will almost always be a potential attraction to an old, unhonoured person like myself. (I don't *think* we have a hanging participle in the previous sentence.) And lascivious thoughts, albeit occasional ones, are not wholly alien even from such a dryasdustest man as me.

"Where are we then? Ah, yes. I went. I went through the doors that had been clearly labelled for my attention, and I knew where I was going; I knew exactly. It will be of little value to you to have a comprehensive account of subsequent events, although (to be fair to myself) they were not particularly sordid. The whole drama (I must admit it) was played with a carefully rehearsed verisimilitude, with myself acting a role that was equally carefully rehearsed. Yet at one stage (if I may continue the metaphor), I forgot my lines completely. And so, perhaps, would you have done. For a devastatingly lovely woman—a Siren fit to beguile the wily Ulysses himself—was almost, *almost* able to rob me of my robe of honour; and, perhaps more importantly, to rob me of my one defence—an army revolver which I had kept since my days in the desert, and which was even now still bulging reassuringly in my jacket-pocket.

"But again things are getting out of sequence, and we must go back. Who was the man I had seen on Staircase T at Lonsdale College? You will have to know. Yes, I am afraid you will have to know.

"I was a young officer in the desert during the battle of El Alamein. I was, I think, a good officer, in the sense that I tried to look after the men in my charge, left little to needless chance, enforced the orders I was given and faced the enemy with the conviction that this conflict—this one, surely—was as fully justified as any in the annals of Christendom. But I knew one thing that no one else could know. I knew that at heart I was a physical coward; and I always feared the thought that, if there were to come a time when I should be called upon to show a personal, an individual—as against a communal, corporate—act of courage, well, I knew that I would fail. And that moment came. And I failed. It came—I need not relate the shameful details—when a man pleaded with me to risk my own life in trying to save the life of a man who was trapped in a fiercely-burning tank. But enough of that. It hurts me deeply, even now, to recall my cowardice.

"Let us now switch forward again. It was all phoney: I soon began to realize that. There were those two bottles of everything, for example: two of them—in whatever the client (in this case, me) should happen to indulge. Why two? The one of them about two-thirds empty (or is it one-third full?); the other completely intact, with the plastic seal fixed round its top. Why go, then, to the new bottle for the first, perfunctory drinks? I didn't know, but I soon began to wonder. And then her accent! Oh dear! Had she been at an audition, any director worth a tuppence of salt would have told her to flush her Gallic vowels down the nearest ladies' lavatory. And then at one point she opened her handbag—a handbag she must have owned for twenty years. A professional whore with an aged handbag? And not only that. She was introduced to me by an unconvincing old hag as 'Yvonne'; so why are the faded gilt initials on the inside flap of her handbag clearly printed 'W. S.'? You see where all this suspicion is leading? But I had my revolver. I was going to be all right. I was all right. (How I hate underlining words in typescript—but often it is necessary.) It was only when this lovely girl (oh dear, she was lovely!) poured my final drink from the other bottle (not the bottle I had drunk from before) that I knew exactly what my situation was. I asked her to open the curtains a little, and whilst she was doing this I poured the (doubtless doctored) contents of my glass inside my trousers, in order that the impression should be given that I had been incapable of controlling myself. (I know you will understand the sense of what, so

delicately, I have tried to express.) You must understand
that at this point she was quite openly and wantonly naked,
and I myself quite justifiably aroused.

"After that? If I may say so, I performed my part professionally. Making vaguely somnolent noises, I now as-
sumed the role of a man (as the Americans have it) in a
totally negative response situation. Then the woman left
me; and after hearing whispered communications on the
other side of the door, I sensed that someone else was in the
room. Let us leave it there.

"I am getting tired with this lengthy typing, but it is
important that I should go on a little longer.

"You were a fool when you were an undergraduate—
wasting, as you did, the precious talent of a clear, clean
mind. It was me (or do you prefer 'I'?) who marked some of
your Greats papers, and even amidst the widespread evidence of your appalling ignorance there were moments of
rare perception and sensitivity. But since that time you
have made a distinguished reputation for yourself as a man
of the Detective (as Dickens has it), and I was anxious that it
should be a worthy brain that was to be pitted against my
own. Why else should the body be discovered where it was?
Who made sure that it should be found at Thrupp—a place
almost in your own back-yard? You will, I suspect, have almost certainly discovered by now why I was not able to
leave the head and the hands for your inspection? Yes, I
think so. You would have been quite certain that it was not
my body had I done so, and I wished to sharpen up your
brain, for (believe me!) it will need to be as sharp as the
sword of Achilles before your work is finished. Here then is
a chance for you to show the sort of quality that was apparent in your early days at Oxford. Perhaps this case of yours
will afford for you the opportunity to kill an ancient ghost,
since I shall quite certainly (albeit posthumously) award you
a 'first' this time if you can grasp the inevitable (and
basically so simple) logic of all these strange events.

"I shall make no further communication to you; and I
advise you not to try to track me down, for you will not find me.

"<u>Post Scriptum</u>. I have just read this letter through and
wish to apologize for the profusion of brackets. (I am not
often over-influenced by the work of Bernard Levin.)"

CHAPTER
TWENTY-THREE

Monday, 28th July

*Investigations proceed with a nominal line drawn
down the middle of needful enquiries.*

So many clues now, and as Morse and Lewis saw things
there were four main areas of enquiry:

1. What were the real facts about that far-off day
   in the desert when Browne-Smith had faced
   his one real test of character—and (apparently)
   failed so lamentably?
2. Where exactly did Westerby (a name cropping
   up repeatedly now) fit into the increasingly
   complex pattern?
3. Who was the person whom Browne-Smith had
   met after his anti-climactic sexual encounter
   with the pseudonymous 'Yvonne'?
4. And (still, to Morse the most vital question of
   all) whose was the body they had found?

Obviously the strands of these enquiries would inter-
weave at many points; but it seemed sensible to the two
detectives that each should make his own investigations for
a day or two, with Lewis concentrating his attentions on the
first two areas, and Morse on the second two.

Lewis spent most of the morning on the telephone,
ringing, amongst other numbers, those of the War Office,
the Ministry of Defence, the HQ of the Wiltshire Reg-

iment, and the Territorial Unit at Devizes. It was a long, frustrating business; but by lunch-time he had a great deal of information, much of it useless, but some of it absolutely vital.

First, he discovered more about Browne-Smith: Captain, acting Major (Royal Wiltshires); served North Africa (1941–42); wounded El Alamein; Italy (1944–45); awarded the MC (1945).

Second, he learned something about Gilbert. There had been three Gilbert brothers, Albert, Alfred, and John. All had fought at El Alamein; the first two, both full corporals, had survived the campaign (although both of them had been wounded); the third, the youngest brother, had died in the same campaign. That was all.

But it couldn't be quite all, Lewis knew that. And it was from the Swindon branch of the British Legion that he learned the address of a man in the Wiltshires who must certainly have known the Gilbert brothers fairly well. Immediately after lunch, Lewis was driving out along the A420.

"Yes, I knew 'em, sergeant—'s funny, I wur a sergeant, too, you know. Yes, there wur Alf 'n Bert—like as two peas in a pod, they wur. One of 'em, 'e got a bit o' the ol' shrapnel in the leg, and I 'ad a bit in the 'ead. We wur at base 'ospital for a while together, but I can't quite recolleck. . . . Real lads, they wur—the pair of 'em!"

"Did you know the other one?" asked Lewis.

"Johnny! That wur 'is name. I didn't know 'im very well, though."

"You don't know how he was killed?"

"No, I don't."

"They were all tank-drivers, weren't they?"

"All of 'em—like me."

"Was he killed in his tank?"

For the second time the old soldier looked rather vague and puzzled, and Lewis wondered whether the man's memory could be relied upon.

"There wur a bit of an accident as I recolleck. But 'e

wurn't with us that morning, sergeant—not when we all moved up 'long Kidney Ridge."

"You don't remember what sort of accident?"

"No. It wur back at base, I seem to. . . . But you get a lot of accidents in wartime, sergeant. More'n they tell the folk back 'ome in Blighty."

He was an engaging old boy; a sixty-nine-year-old widower for whom, it seemed, the war had been the only intermission of importance in a largely anonymous life, for there was no real sadness in him as he recalled those weeks and months of fighting in the desert—only an almost understandable nostalgia. So Lewis wrote down the facts, such as they were, in his painstakingly slow long-hand, and then took his leave.

Morse was away from the office when Lewis returned at 4:30 p.m. and of this fact he was strangely glad. All the way back from Swindon he had been wondering what that "accident" might have been. He suspected that had Morse been there he would have guessed immediately; and it was a pleasant change to be able to tackle the problem at his own, rather slower, pace. He rang the War Office once again, was put through to the Archives section, and soon began to realize that he was on to something important.

"Yes, we might be able to help in some way. You're Thames Valley Police, you say?"

"That's right."

"Why are you asking for information about this man?"

"It's in connection with a murder, sir."

"I see. What's your number? Can't be too careful in these things—you'll know all about that." He spoke with the monotone bark of a machine-gun.

So Lewis gave him his number, was rung back inside thirty seconds, and was given an extraordinary piece of information. Private John Gilbert of the Royal Wiltshires had not been killed in the El Alamein campaign. He had played no part in it. The night before the offensive, he had taken his army rifle, placed the muzzle inside his mouth, and shot himself through the brain. The incident had been hushed up on the highest orders; and that for obvious reasons. A

few had known, of course—*had* to know. But "officially" John
Gilbert died on active service in the desert, and that is how
his family and his friends had been informed.

"This is all in the strictest confidence, you understand
that?"

"Of course, sir."

"Never good for morale, that sort of thing, eh?"

Morse was having a far less fruitful day. He realized
that with the first of his self-imposed assignments he could
for the present make little headway, since that would neces-
sitate some far from disagreeable investigations in Soho—a
journey he had planned for the morrow. Which only left
him with the same old tantalizing problem that had monop-
olized his mind from the beginning: the identity of the
corpse. From the embarrassment of clues contained in
Browne-Smith's letter, the shortest odds must now be
surely on the man whom Browne-Smith had finally encountered in London. But who was that man? Had it been
Gilbert, as the letter so obviously suggested? Or was the
body *Westerby's*? If Browne-Smith had killed anyone, then
Westerby was surely the most likely of candidates. Or was
the body that of someone who had not yet featured in the
investigations? Some outsider? Someone as yet unknown
who would make a dramatic entry only towards the finale of
Act Five? A sort of *deus ex machina*? Morse doubted this
last possibility—and amidst his doubts, quite suddenly the
astonishing thought flashed through his mind that there
might just be a *fourth* possibility. And the more Morse pondered the idea, the more he convinced himself that there
was: the possibility that the puffed and sodden salt-white
corpse was that of *Dr. Browne-Smith*.

On the way home that evening, Lewis decided to risk
his wife's wrath, to face the prospect of almost certainly re-
heated chips—and to call on Simon Rowbotham in Botley.

Simon Rowbotham invited him into the small terraced
house in which he lived with his mother. But Lewis declined, learning over the doorstep that Simon had been one
of three anglers who had spotted the body, and that it was

he, Simon, who had readily volunteered to dial the police in lieu of looking further upon the horror just emerging from the waters. He often fished out along the banks at Thrupp, a good place for specialists such as himself. As it happened, they were just about to form a new angling club there, for which he had volunteered his services as secretary. In fact (just as Lewis had called) he had been checking a proof of the new association's letter-head for the printer. They had managed to persuade a few well known people to support them; and clearly, for Simon Rowbotham, the world was entering an exciting phase.

Lewis waited until 8:30 p.m. before ringing Morse (who had been strangely absent somewhere since lunchtime). He found him at his flat and promptly reported on his day's work.

When he had finished, Morse could hardly keep the excitement out of his voice. "Just go over that bit about John Gilbert again, will you, Lewis?"

So Lewis repeated, as accurately as he could recall it, the news he had gleaned from the War-Office archivist; and he felt very happy as he did so, for he knew that the news was pleasing to his master—a master, incidentally, who now had guessed the whole truth about the desert episode.

"You've done a marvellous day's work, old friend. Well done!"

"Did *you* find out anything new, sir?"

"Me? Well, yes and no, really. I've—I've been thinking about the case for most of the day. But nothing startling."

"Anyway, have a good day in London tomorrow, sir!"

"What? Ah yes—tomorrow. I'll—er—give you a ring if I find out anything exciting."

"Perhaps you'll do that, sir."

"What? Ah yes—perhaps I will."

A rather sad footnote to the events described in this chapter is that if Lewis had been slightly more interested in the formation of a new angling association and if he had asked to see the proof of the proposed letter-heading (but why should he?), he would have found that one of the two honorary vice-presidents listed at the top left-hand corner of the page was a man with a name which was now very familiar to him: Mr. G. Westerby (Lonsdale College, Oxford).

CHAPTER TWENTY-FOUR

Tuesday, 29th July

Morse appears to have a powerful effect on two women, one of whom he has never met.

For Lewis, a 10 a.m. visit to Lonsdale was pleasantly productive, since the college secretary (she liked Lewis) had brought him a cup of coffee, and been quite willing to talk openly about Westerby as a person. So Lewis made his notes. Then he found out something about *cars*, since—in spite of Morse's apparent indifference to the problem—it seemed to him of great importance to discover exactly how the corpse had been transported from London to Thrupp; and he learned that Browne-Smith—doubtless on doctor's orders—had sold his Daimler a month or so ago, whilst Westerby still ran a red Metro, occasionally to be seen in the college forecourt.

"Why would Westerby want a car, though?" asked Lewis. "He lived in college."

"I don't know. He's a bit secretive—doesn't tell anyone much about what he does."

"He must go *somewhere*?"

"I suppose so," she nodded vaguely.

"Nice little car, the Metro. Economical!"

"Roomy in the back, too. You can take the seats out, you know—get no end of stuff in there."

"So they tell me, yes."

"You've got a car, sergeant?"

"I've got an old Mini, but I don't use it much. Usually go to work on the bus and then use a police car."

The college secretary looked down at her desk. "Has Inspector Morse got a car?"

Lewis found it an odd question. "He's got a Lancia. He's had a Lancia ever since I've known him."

"You've known him long?"

"Long enough."

"Is he a nice man?"

"Well, I wouldn't exactly call him 'nice.'"

"Do you like him?"

"I don't think you 'like' Morse. He's not that sort of person, really."

"But you get on well with him?"

"Usually. You see—well, he's the most remarkable man I've ever met, that's all."

"He must think *you're* a remarkable man—if he works with you all the time, I mean."

"No! I'm just, well. . . ." Lewis didn't quite know how to finish, but he felt more than a little pride in the shadow of the compliment. "Do you know him, then, Miss?"

She shook her pretty head. "He spoke to me over the phone once, that's all."

"Oh, he's terrible over the phone—always sounds so, I don't know, so cocky and nasty, somehow."

"You mean . . . he's not *really* like that?"

"Not really," said Lewis quietly. Then he noticed that the gentle eyes of the college secretary had suddenly drifted away from himself, and out towards a man she had never known or even seen. Momentarily he felt a twinge of jealousy.

Morse!

Down the dingy red-carpeted stairs, through the dingy red curtains, Morse, at 11 a.m., followed the same path that Browne-Smith had trodden eighteen days before him. He sat at a table in the Flamenco Topless Bar, and transacted his business with a milky-white maiden. It didn't take him long; and, after that, Browne-Smith's spunky antagonist behind the bar had proved no match for him, since for some reason she could not conceive of suggesting to *this* man, with the blue-grey eyes and the thinning, grey-black hair, that he could go across the way to the Sauna if he wanted any further sexual gratification. He seemed to her coldly detached; and when he looked at her with eyes intensely still, she found herself answering his questions almost hypnotically. Thus it was that Morse, in a short space of time, had penetrated the door marked "Private" at the rear of the drinking lounge.

At 1 p.m. he was riding in a taxi to an address he had known anyway—the address already pencilled firmly in his mind when that same morning he had left the Number One platform at Oxford on the 9:12 train. Perhaps he should have short-circuited the whole process; but on the whole he thought not, even though he had felt not the vaguest stir of virility as one of the girls had sat opposite him, sipping her exotic juice.

So far so good; and comparatively easy. The outlines of the pattern had been confirmed at every stage: Gilbert (one of twins, as Lewis had told him—interesting!) had quite fortuitously found a client in Oxford; and opposite his client's room he'd seen, in Gothic script, a name that for some reason was indelibly printed on his mind; with (doubtless) considerable ingenuity, he had lured this man to London— lured him to the address which Morse had just given to his taxi-driver, the same address that Morse had memorized from the wooden crates in the rooms of Westerby on Staircase T: 29 Cambridge Way, London, WC1. But what had happened after the suspicious and resourceful Browne-Smith had faced his *second* test of personal courage? What exactly had occurred when "Yvonne" had left . . . and someone else had entered?

Such thoughts occupied Morse's mind as the taxi made its way (by an extremely circuitous route, it seemed to Morse) to Cambridge Way. Yet there were other thoughts, too: he could, of course, claim full expenses for his train fare (first class, although he usually travelled second), tube fare, taxi fare, subsistence. . . . Yes, he might *just* make enough on the day to settle down happily in the buffet car on his return and enjoy a couple of Scotches at someone else's expense. But would he be justified in sticking down on his claims-form such a ludicrous-looking item as "Flamenco Revenge—£6"? On the whole, he thought, probably not.

He alighted, and stood alone in front of Number 29.

CHAPTER
TWENTY-FIVE

Tuesday, 29th July

*Lewis retraces some of his steps, and makes some
startling new discoveries.*

Lewis was back at Police HQ by 11:30 a.m., sensing
that without further directions from on high he had gone as
far as he was likely to go. But just for the moment he felt a
little resentful about taking too many orders; and by noon
he had taken the firm decision to revisit the scene of the
crime. He didn't quite know why.

After drinking half a pint of bitter in the Boat Inn, he
walked out along the road by the canal and up to Aubrey's
Bridge. But there were no fishermen there this morning,
and he turned his attention to his left as he walked slowly
along, noting once more the authoritative notices posted
regularly along the low, neat terrace: "No mooring opposite
these cottages." The people here were obviously jealous of
their acquired territories—doubtless rich enough, too, to
own boats of their own and to regard it as some divine right
that they should moor such craft immediately opposite their
neatly-painted porches.

Then something stirred in Lewis's mind. . . . If all
these people were so anxious to preserve their rights and
their privacy; if all those sharp eyes there were jealously
watching the waterfront for the first signs of any territorial
trespass—then, surely, in this quiet cul-de-sac that led to
nowhere, where there was hardly room enough to execute a
six-point turn in a car . . . yes! Surely, someone must have

seen something? For the body must quite certainly have been pushed into the canal from the back of a car. How else? And yet Lewis, who had himself earlier questioned the tenants, had learned nothing of any strange car. Understandably, not every cottage had been inhabited at the time; the owners of some had been away—boating, or shopping in Oxford, or waiting in high places in large cities to motor down for a weekend of rural relaxation in their quiet country cottages.

Lewis had now reached the end of his walk, looking down as he did so at the water wherein the hideous body had been found. From his perusal he learned nothing. As he made his way back, however, he saw that the third cottage from the far end was "For Sale," and he began to wonder whether such a property might not perhaps make a nice little investment for himself and the missus when he retired. Retired. . . . And suddenly an exciting thought occurred to him. He knocked loudly on the door of the house for sale. No answer. Then he knocked at the house next door, which was opened by a freckle-faced lad of about twelve years of age.

"Is your mum in—or your dad?"

"No."

"I was just trying to find out something about the house here." Lewis pointed to the empty property.

"They want twenny thousand forrit—and it's got a leaky roof."

"Lot of money," said Lewis.

"Not worth it. It's been on the market a couple of months."

Lewis nodded, sizing up this embryo property-evaluator. "You live here?"

The boy nodded.

"Did you know the people next door—before it was for sale?"

"Not 'people.'"

"No?"

The young lad looked vaguely suspicious, but he blinked and agreed: "No."

"Look!" said Lewis. "I'm a policeman and—"

"I know. I saw you when you was here before."

"Shouldn't you have been at school?"

"I had the measles, didn't I? I was watching from the bedroom."

"You didn't see anything sort of suspicious—before that, I mean?"

The boy shook his head.

"You say it wasn't 'people' next door?"

"He's not in any trouble, is he?" The freckled face looked up at Lewis anxiously, as if it were a matter of deep concern to him that any trouble might have befallen the previous owner of the house next door.

"Not so far as I know."

The boy looked down at the threshold and spoke quietly: "He was good to me. Took me out in his Metro to King's Weir, once. Super fisherman he was—Mr. Westerby."

A Jaguar's horn blared imperiously as Lewis turned left on to the main road down to Kidlington, and he knew his mind was full of other things. He had just discovered a quite extraordinarily significant link between Westerby and the waterfront at Thrupp. And if someone had taken a body from London to Thrupp in a car (as someone must have done), there would have been no suspicions aroused by the familiar sight of a red Metro. No trouble at all. Not if that someone who had brought the body *had lived there himself.* What was more, this was the only car that had cropped up in the case so far, for Dr. Browne-Smith had sold his large, black Daimler. . . .

Lewis turned into HQ and sat down at Morse's desk, giving his bubbling thoughts the chance to simmer down. The green box-file containing the few documents on the case was lying open before him, and he riffled through the sheets—most of them his own reports. In fact (he told himself) there were only two *real* clues, anyway, whatever anyone might say: the suit, and the torn letter. Yes . . . and that torn letter was here, in his hands now—together with Morse's neatly-written reconstruction of the whole. He looked down at the torn half once more, and the final "G" in line 7 and the final "J" in line 15 suddenly shot out at him from the page. *Could* it be?

He parked the police car half on the pavement outside the Examination Schools and felt like a nervous punter in a betting-shop who can hardly bear to read the latest 1, 2, 3. The lists were still posted around the entrance hall, and quickly he found the board announcing the final honours list for Geography and read through the names. Whew! It not only could be—it *was*. "Jennifer Bennet." There she perched at the top of the list—that wonderful girl beginning with "J" whom he had found on a board beginning with "G." And the college—Lonsdale. Lewis could hardly believe his eyes, or his luck. And there was more to come, for the bottom name of the examining sextet was none other than Westerby's!

It was an excited Lewis who drove back to Kidlington; but, even as he drove, the conflicting nature of his morning's findings was slowly becoming apparent to him. Most of what he had discovered was pointing with an insistent regularity in one direction—in the direction of George Westerby. And with Browne-Smith as the body and Westerby as the murderer, almost everything fitted the facts beautifully. Except . . . except that last bit. Because if the letter had been written to *Westerby*, and not to Browne-Smith . . . oh dear! Lewis was beginning to feel a little lost. He wondered if Morse had spent such a successful morning in London. He doubted it—doubted it genuinely. But how he longed to talk to Morse!

Back in the office, Lewis typed up his findings and although spelling had never been Lewis's strong suit, yet he felt rather pleased with his present reports, particularly with his little vignette of Westerby:

Londoner. Little dapper bumshious fellow— slightly deaf—pretty secretive. Tends to squint a bit, but this may be the usual cigarette at the corner of his mouth.

CHAPTER TWENTY-SIX

Tuesday, 29th July

Unable to get any answer from the house in Cambridge Way, Morse now reflects upon his meeting with the manager of the Flamenco Topless Bar.

Like Browne-Smith before him, Morse walked slowly up the shallow steps of Number 29 and rang the bell. But he, too, heard no sound of ringing on the other side of the great black door. He rang again, noticing as he did so the same board that Browne-Smith must have seen, with its invitation to apply to "Brooks & Gilbert (Sole Agents)." Almost imperceptibly he nodded; almost imperceptibly he smiled. But there was still no sign of any movement in the house, and he bent down to look through the highly polished brass letter-box. He could make out the light-olive carpeting on the wide staircase that faced him; but the place seemed ominously silent. He walked across the street and looked up at the four-storied building, admiring the clean-cut architecture, and the progressively foreshortened oblongs of the window-frames, behind which—as far as he could see—there was not the slightest tell-tale twitching of the curtainings. So he walked away along the street, entered a small park, and sat down on a bench, where he communed for many minutes with the pigeons, and with his thoughts. On the taxi-journey he had sought in his mind to minimize the risks he had already run that morning; and yet, as he now began to realize, those risks had been decidedly dangerous, especially after he had walked through the door marked "Private" . . .

He'd started off in the quiet monotone of a man whose
authority was beyond that of other men: "It matters to me
not a single fart in the cosmos, lad, whether you tell me
about it here and now, or in one of the cells of Her Majesty's
nearest nick."

"I don't know who the bloody hell you think you are,
talking to me like that. Let me tell you——"

"Before you tell me anything, just call in one of your
tarts out there, preferably the one with the biggest tits, and
tell her to bring me a large Scotch, preferably Bell's. On the
house, I suggest—because I'm here to *help* you, lad."

"I was going to tell you that I've got friends here who'd
gladly kick the guts out of the likes of you."

"'Friends,' you say?"

"Yeah—friends!"

"If you mean what you say, lad, I don't honestly think
they're going to thank you very much if you bring *them* into
this little business—and get 'em involved with *me*."

"They're one helluva sight tougher than you, mate!"

"Oh no! You've got it all wrong, lad. And one little
thing. You can curse and swear as much as you like with me,
but you must never call me 'mate' again! Is that understood? I've told you who I am, and I shan't be telling you
again."

The manager swallowed hard. "I suppose you're going
to tell me you've got a van full of squaddies outside. Is that
it?"

Morse allowed a vague smile to form at the corners of
his mouth. "No, that's not it. I'm here completely on my
own—and what's more no one else knows I'm here at all.
Well, let's be honest, *almost* no one. And if we get along,
you and me, I shan't even tell anyone that I've been here,
either. No need really, is there?"

The manager was biting down hard on the nail of his
left index finger, and Morse pressed home his obvious advantage.

"Let me give you a bit of advice. You're not a crook—
you're not in the same league as most of the murderous
morons I deal with every day. And, even if you were, I
wouldn't need a posse of police to go around protecting *me*.

You know why, lad?" Morse broke off for a few seconds, before focusing his eyes with almost manic ferocity upon the youngish man seated opposite him. Then he shook his head almost sorrowfully. "No, you don't know why, do you? So let me tell you. It's because the archangels look after me, lad—always have done. And most especially when I'm pursuing my present calling as the protector of Law and eternal Justice!" Morse managed to give each of these mighty personages a capital letter; and pompous as he sounded, he also sounded very frightening.

Certainly, this was the impact upon the manager, for he appeared now to have little faith that he would be likely to emerge victorious from any conflict with the archangelic trio. He walked to the door, and sounded suddenly resigned as he asked "Racquel" to fetch two double-Scotches; whilst, for a rather frightened Morse, the prospect of finding himself dead or dying in a Soho side-street was gradually receding.

The manager's story was brief.

The club was registered in the name of Soho Enterprises Limited, although he had never himself met anyone (or so he thought) directly from this syndicate. Business was transacted through a soberly-dressed intermediary—a Mr. Schwenck—who periodically visited the bar to look around, and who collected takings and paid all salaries. About three weeks or so ago (he couldn't remember exactly), Mr. Schwenck had announced that a certain Mr. William would very soon be calling; that the said Mr. William would make his requests known, and that no questions were to be asked. In fact, the bearded Mr. William had requested very little, spurning equally the offers of hospitality from the bar and from the bra-less hostesses. He had taken away a projector and two reels of pornographic film, and announced that he would be back the following morning. And he had been, bringing with him a small blue card (given to the manager) and a cassette of some piano music (given to the girl behind the bar). Thereafter he had stood quietly at the bar, reading a paperback and drinking half a glass of lime-juice. Another man (so the manager had been informed) would probably be coming in that morning;

and at some point this newcomer would be directed to the office where he was to be given the blue card, plus an address. That was all.

The young man appeared not overtly dishonest (albeit distinctly uncomfortable) as he told his little tale; and Morse found himself believing him.

"How much in it for you?" he asked.

"Nothing. I'm only—"

"Couple of hundred?"

"I told you—?"

"Five hundred?"

"What? Just for—?"

"Forget it, lad! What was on the card?"

"Nothing really. It was just one of those cards that— that let you into places."

"Which place?"

"I—I don't remember."

"You didn't write it down?"

"No. I remembered it."

"You've got a good memory?"

"Good enough."

"But you just said you *can't* remember."

"I can't. It was a good while ago now."

"When exactly was it?"

"I can't—"

"Friday? Friday 11th July?"

"Could have been."

"Did you get your projector and stuff back all right?"

"'Course I did."

"The next day?"

"Yes—er—I think it was the next day."

For the first time Morse felt convinced that the man was lying. But why (Morse asked himself) should the man have lied to him on *that* particular point?

"About that address. Was it a number in Cambridge Way by any chance?"

Morse noted the dart of recognition in the manager's eyes, and was about to repeat his question when the telephone rang. The manager pounced on the receiver, clamping it closely to his right ear.

"Yes" (Morse could hear nothing of the caller's voice) "Yes" (a quick, involuntary look across at Morse) "Yes" (unease, quite certainly, in the manager's eyes) "All right" (sudden relief in the manager's face?).

Morse's hand flashed across the table and snatched the receiver, but he heard only the dull, quiet purr of the dialling tone.

"Only the wife, inspector. She wants me to take five pounds of potatoes home. Run out, she says. You know how these women are."

Something had happened, Morse knew that. The young manager had got a shot of confidence from somewhere, and Morse began to wonder whether his patrons, Michael, Raphael and Gabriel, might not, after all, be called upon to fight his cause. He heard the door open quietly behind him—but not to admit the roundly bosomed Racquel with a further double-Scotch. In the doorway stood a diminutive Chinaman of about thirty years of age, his brown arms under the white, short-sleeved shirt as sleek and sinewy as the limbs of a Derby favourite in the Epsom paddock. It seemed to Morse a little humiliating to be cowed into instant submission by such a hominid; but Morse was. He rose to his feet, averted his gaze from the twin slits of horizontal hostility in the Chinaman's face, and thanked the manager civilly for his co-operation, rueing the fact that he was himself now far too decrepit even to enlist in the kung-fu classes advertised weekly in the *Oxford Times*. But the Chinaman guided him gently back to his chair; and it was more than half an hour (a period, however, of unmolested confinement) before Morse was allowed to leave the Topless Bar, whence he emerged into the upper world just after 1 p.m., deeply and gratefully inhaling the foul fumes of the cars that circled Piccadilly Circus, and crossing carefully to its west side, where he had a wait of only two minutes outside the Café Royal before a taxi pulled up in front of him.

"Where to, guv?"

Morse told him, infinitely preferring "guv" to "mate."

CHAPTER
TWENTY-SEVEN

Tuesday, 29th July, p.m.

In which Morse views a luxury block of flats in central London, catching an enigmatic glimpse of one of its tenants and looking longer upon our second corpse.

Morse had been sitting over half an hour, pondering these and other things, when the extraordinary thought crossed his mind that he was in the middle of a park in the middle of opening hours with a pub only fifty yards away on the corner of the square. Yet somehow he sensed that events were gathering pace, and he walked past the Duke of Cambridge, went up the steps of Number 29, and rang the bell once more. This time he was in luck, for after a couple of minutes the great black door was opened.

"Yis, guv?"

He was a mournful-looking man in his mid-sixties, sweating slightly, wearing a beige-coloured working overall, carrying a caretaker's long-handled floor-mop, and fiddling with the controls of a stringed, National Health hearing-aid.

Morse explained who he was and, upon producing his identification, was reluctantly admitted across the threshold. The man (announcing himself as Hoskins—pronounced 'oskins) informed Morse that he had been the porter in the flats for just over a year now: 8:45 a.m. to 4:30 p.m., Tuesdays to Fridays, his job consisting mainly of keeping an eye on the properties and doing a bit of general cleaning during working hours. "Nice little job, guv."

149

"Still some flats for sale, I see?"

"No—not nah. Both of 'em sold. Should 'a' taken the notice darn, really—still, it's good for business, I s'pose."

"*Both* of them sold?"

"Yis, guv. One of 'em's a gent from Oxford—bought it a coupla months back, 'e did."

"And the other one?"

"Few days ago. Some foreign gent, I think it is."

"The one from Oxford—that's Mr. Westerby, isn't it?"

"You know 'im, then?"

"Is he in?"

"No. I 'aven't seen 'im since 'e came to look rarnd, like." The man hesitated. "Nuffin wrong, is there?"

"Everything's wrong, Mr. Hoskins, I'm afraid. You'd better show me round his flat, if you will."

Rather laboriously the man led the way up the stairs to the first floor, produced a key from his overall pocket, and opened the door across from the landing with the apprehension of a man who expects to cast his eye upon a carpet swimming with carnage. But the pale-grey carpeting in the small (and otherwise completely unfurnished) anteroom provided evidence only of a recent, immaculate hoovering.

"Main room's through there, guv."

Inside this second room, half a dozen pieces of heavy, mahogany furniture stood at their temporary sites around the walls, whilst the floor space was more than half covered by oblong wooden crates, several piled on top of others—crates each labeled neatly with the name and new address of a G. O. Westerby, Esq., MA; crates which Morse had recognized immediately, especially the one, already opened, which had contained the head of Gerardus Mercator (now standing on the mantelpiece).

"Mr. Westerby already been here?"

"Not seen 'im, guv. But o' course, 'e might 'a' come later—after I was off. Looks like it, don't it?"

Morse nodded, looking aimlessly around the room, and then trying the two fitted wardrobes, both of which were unlocked, empty, dusty. And Morse frowned, knowing that somewhere something was wrong. He pointed back to the ante-room. "Did you hoover the carpet in there?"

The man's face (Morse could have sworn it) had paled a few degrees. "No—I just, as I said, look after the general cleaning, like—stairs and that sort o' thing."

But Morse sensed that the man was lying, and found no difficulty in guessing why: a caretaker in a block of flats like this . . . half a dozen wealthy and undomesticated men . . . a few nice little backhanders now and again just to dust and to clean . . . Yes, Morse could imagine the picture all right; and it might well be that a caretaker in such a block of flats would know rather more about one or two things than he was prepared to admit. Yet Morse was singularly unsuccessful in eliciting even the slightest piece of information, and he changed the course of his questioning.

"Did *you* show Mr. Westerby round here?"

"No, chap from the agents, it was—young fellow."

"Always the same young fellow, is it?"

"Pardon, sir?"

"You say they've just sold the other flat?"

"Ah I see. No, I wasn't 'ere then."

"It's not Mr. Gilbert himself, is it—this young fellow you mention?"

"I wouldn't know—I never met 'im personally, like."

"I see." Again Morse sensed that the man was holding something back, and again he aimed blindly in the dark. "You know when Mr. Westerby called again . . . when was it, about a week, ten days ago?"

"I told you, sir. I only saw 'im the once—the day 'e looked rarnd the place."

"I see." But Morse saw nothing, apart from the fact that far from hitting any bull's eye he'd probably missed the target altogether. Without any clear purpose he proceeded to look into the small kitchen, and then into the bathroom; but the only thing that mildly registered in his mind was that the parquet flooring in each was sparklingly clean, and he felt quite convinced now that Hoskins (almost certainly in contravention of his contract) was working a very profitable little fiddle for himself with his mop and his cleansing-fluid.

So it was that slowly and disconsolately Morse followed what he now saw as the marginally devious little caretaker down the broad staircase towards the front door. And at that point, had it not been for one fortuitous occurrence, perhaps the simple yet quite astounding truth of the present case might never have beached upon the shores of light. For Morse had heard a lift descending, and now he saw a dark-skinned, grey-suited man emerge from the side of the entrance-hall.

"Arternoon, sir," said Hoskins, touching some imaginary lock on his balding pate.

The affluent-looking Arab was walking in the opposite direction from the front door, and as he watched him Morse whispered to his companion: "Where's *he* going?"

"There's a back entrance 'ere, guv. . . ."

But Morse hardly heard, for the Arab himself had looked over his shoulder, and was in turn looking back towards Morse with a puzzled, vaguely worried frown.

"Who's he?" asked Morse very quietly.

"'e lives on the—"

But again Morse was not listening, for his thoughts were travelling via the unsuspected lift towards the higher storeys. "He finishes work early, doesn't he?"

"'e can afford to, guv."

"Yes. Like you can, sometimes, Hoskins! Take me up to the flat that's just been sold!"

The small but extraordinarily efficient lift brought them swiftly up to the top storey, where Hoskins nervously fingered a bouquet of silvery keys, finally finding the correct one, and pushing open the door for the policeman to enter.

Things were at last falling into place in Morse's mind, and as they stood by the opened door his aim was more deliberate.

"Did they give you the afternoon off, Hoskins?"

"What afternoon, guv?" the man protested. But not for long.

It had been on the Friday, he confessed. He'd had a phone call, and been given a couple of fivers—huh!—just for staying away from the place.

Morse was nodding to himself as he entered the rooms. Yes . . . the Gilbert twins: one of them a housing agent; the other a removals man. Sell some property—and recommend a highly reputable and efficient removals firm; buy some property—and also recommend the same paragon of pantechniconic skills. Very convenient, and very profitable. Over the years the two brothers must have worked a neatly dovetailed little business. . . .

Now, again, Morse looked around him at a potentially luxurious flat in central London: the small entrance hall, the living room, the bedroom, the kitchen, the bathroom— all newly decorated. No carpets yet, though; no curtains, either. But there was not a flick of cigarette ash, not even a forgotten tintack, on the light-oak boards, as spotless as those of an army barrack floor before the CO's inspection.

"You've been cleaning in here, too?" asked Morse.

The walls were professionally painted in lilac emulsion, the doors and fitted cupboards in brilliant-white gloss. And Morse, suddenly thinking back to his own bachelor flat with the heavy old walnut suite his mother had left him, began to envisage some lighter, brighter, modernistic furniture for himself as he opened one of the fitted wardrobes in the bedroom with its inbuilt racks and airy, deep recesses. And not just one of them!

But the second one was locked.

"You got the key for this, Hoskins?"

"No, sir. I only keep the keys for the doors. If people wants to lock things up. . . ."

"Let's look in the kitchen!"

Beside the sink, Morse found a medium-sized screwdriver, the only object of any kind abandoned (it seemed) by the previous owner.

"Think this'll open it, Hoskins?"

"I—I don't want to get you in any trouble, sir—or me. I shouldn't really 'ave. . . . I just don't think it's right to mess up the place and damage things, sir."

(The "sirs" were coming thick and fast.)

It was time, Morse thought, for some reassurance. "Look, Hoskins, this is my responsibility. I'm doing my duty as a police officer—you're doing your duty as a good citizen. You understand that?"

The miserable man appeared a modicum mollified and nodded silently. And indeed it was he, after a brief and ineffectual effort from Morse, who proved the more successful; for he managed to insert the screwdriver far enough into the gap between the side of the cupboard door and the surrounding architrave to gain sufficient leverage. Then, with a joint prizing, the lock finally snapped, the wood splintered, and the door swung slowly open. Inside, slumped on the floor of the deep recess, was the body of a man, the head turned towards the wall; and almost exactly halfway between the shoulder-blades was a round hole in the dead man's sports-jacket, from which was oozing still a steady drip of bright-red blood, feeding a darker pool upon the floor. Almost squeamishly, Morse inserted his left hand under the lifeless, lolling head . . . and turned it towards him.

"My God!"

For a few moments the two men stood looking down on the face that stared back up at them with open, bulging eyes.

"Do you know who it is?" croaked Morse.

"I never seen him before, sir. I swear I 'aven't." The man was shaking all over, and Morse noticed the ashen-grey pallor in his cheeks and the beads of sweat upon his forehead.

"Take it easy, old boy!" said Morse in a kindly, understanding voice. "Just tell me where the nearest telephone is—then you'd better get off home for a while. We can always—"

Morse was about to lay a comforting hand upon the man's shoulder; but he was already too late, for now he found another body slumped about his feet.

Five minutes later, after dialling 999 from the telephone in the living-room, and after sending the old boy off home (having elicited a full name and home address from those jibbering lips), Morse stood once again looking down at the corpse in the cupboard recess. A tiny triangle of white card was showing above the top pocket of the jacket, and Morse bent down to extract it. There were a dozen or so similar cards there, but he took only one and read it—his face betraying only the grimmest confirmation. He'd known anyway, because he'd recognized the face immediately. It was the face of the man whom Morse had last (and first) seen in the rooms of George Westerby, Geography don at Lonsdale College, Oxford: the face of A. Gilbert, Esq., late proprietor of the firm Removals Anywhere.

CHAPTER TWENTY-EIGHT

Tuesday, 29th July

Morse meets a remarkable woman, and learns of another woman who might be more remarkable still.

On the left sat a very black gentleman in a very smart pin-striped suit, studying the pink pages of *The Financial Times*; on the right sat a long-haired young brunette, wearing enormous earrings, and reading *Ulysses*; in the middle sat Morse, impatiently fingering a small white oblong card; and all the while the tube-train clattered along the stations on the northbound Piccadilly line.

To Morse it seemed an inordinately long journey, and one during which he found it almost impossible to concentrate his mind. Perhaps it had been improper for him (as the plain-clothes sergeant had diffidently hinted) to have fled the scene of the recent crime so precipitately; quite certainly it had bordered upon the criminally negligent (as the plain-clothes sergeant had more forcefully asserted) that he had allowed the one and only other witness to have left the premises in Cambridge Way—whatever the state of shock that had paralysed the man's frame. But at least Morse had explained where he was going—had even given the address and the telephone number. And he could always do his best to explain, to apologize . . . later.

Arsenal. (Nearly there.)

The brunette's eyes flickered over Morse's face, but flashed back immediately to Bloom, as though the latter were a subject of considerably greater interest.

Finsbury Park. (Next stop.)

Suddenly Morse stiffened bolt upright in his seat, and this time it was the gentleman from the city whose bloodshot eyes turned suspiciously towards his travelling companion, as though he half expected to find a man in the initial throes of an epileptic fit.

That screwdriver . . . and that small, round hole in the middle of those sagging shoulder-blades . . . and he, Morse, a man who had lectured so often on proper procedure in cases of homicide, *he* had just left his own fine set of fingerprints around the bulbous handle of—the murder-weapon! Oh dear! Yes, there might well come, and fairly soon, the time for more than an apology, more than a little explanation.

For the moment, however, Morse was totally convinced that he was right (as indeed for once he was) in recognizing the signs of a tide in the affairs of men that must be taken at the flood; and when he emerged from the underground into the litter-strewn streets of Manor House, he suspected that the gods were smiling happily upon him, for almost immediately he spotted Berrywood Court, a tall tenement block only some hundred yards away down Seven Sisters Road.

Mrs. Emily Gilbert, an unlovely woman in her late fifties (her teeth darkly stained) capitulated quickly to Morse's urgent questioning. She'd known it was all silly; and she'd told her husband it might be dangerous as well. But it was just a joke, he'd said. Some joke! She'd met another woman there in Cambridge Way—an attractive Scandinavian-looking woman who (so Mrs. G. had thought) had been hired from one of the better-class clubs in Soho. They'd both been briefed by Albert (her husband) and—well, that was it really. This man had come to the place, and she (Mrs. G.) had left the pair of them together in a first-floor flat (yes, Mr. Westerby's flat). Then, after an hour or so, Albert had come up to tell her (she was waiting in an empty top-floor flat) that he was very pleased with the way things had gone, that she (Mrs. G.) was a good old girl, and that the odd little episode could now be happily forgotten.

She had a strangely intense and rather pleasing voice, and Morse found himself gradually reassessing her. "This other woman," he asked, "what was her name?"

"I was told to call her 'Yvonne.'"

"She didn't tell you where she lived? Where she worked?"

"No. But she was 'class'—you know what I mean? She was sort of tasteful—beautifully made-up, lovely figure."

"You don't know where she lives?"

"No. Albert'll probably be able to tell you, though."

"Do you know where *he* is, Mrs. Gilbert?"

She shook her head. "In his sort of business you're off all the time. I know he's got a few jobs on in the Midlands—and one in Scotland—but he's always on the move. He just turns up here when he gets back."

At this point, Morse felt a curious compassion for Emily Gilbert, for she seemed to him a brave sort of woman—yet one who would need to be even braver very soon. He knew, too, that time was running out; knew he had to find out more before he broke the cruel news.

"Just tell me anything you can, please, about this other woman—this 'Yvonne.' Anything you can remember."

"I've told you—I don't—"

"Didn't you talk together?"

"Well, yes—but—"

"You don't have any idea where I can find her?"

"I think she lives south of the Thames somewhere."

"No name of the road? No number of the house? Come on! Think, woman!"

But Morse had pushed things too far, for Mrs. Gilbert now broke down and wept, and Morse was at a loss as to what to do, or what to say. So he did nothing; and such masterly inactivity proved to be the prudent course, for very soon she had wiped her wide and pleasing eyes and apologized sweetly for what she called her "silliness."

"Have you any children?" asked Morse.

She shook her head sadly.

It was hardly the most propitious moment, but Morse now rose from the sofa and placed his right hand firmly on her shoulder. "Please be brave, Mrs. Gilbert! I've got to tell you, I'm afraid, that your husband is dead."

With a dramatic, convulsive jerk, her right hand snapped up to meet Morse's, and he felt the sinewy vigour of her fingers as they sought to clutch the comfort of his own. Then Morse told her, in a very quiet, gentle voice, as much (and as little) as he knew.

When he had finished, Mrs. Gilbert asked him no questions, but got up from her chair, walked over to the window, lit a cigarette, and stared out over the long, bleak reservoir that lay below, where a swan glided effortlessly across the still waters. Then, finally, she turned towards him, and for the first time Morse realized that she must have been an adequately attractive woman . . . some few little summers ago. Her eyes, still glistening with tears, sought his.

"I lied to you, inspector, and I shouldn't have done that. I *know* that other woman, you see. My husband occasionally gets—got involved in his brother's—well, let's say his brother's side of things, and he met her in one of the clubs a few weeks ago. I—I found out about it. You see—he wanted to leave me and go and—and go and live with her. But she—"

Mrs. Gilbert broke off, and Morse nodded his understanding.

"But she didn't want him."

"No, she didn't."

"Did you tell him you'd found out?"

Mrs. Gilbert smiled a wan sort of smile and she turned back to the window, her eyes drifting over and beyond the reservoir to where a DC10 droned in towards Heathrow. "No! I wanted to keep him. Funny, isn't it? But he was the only thing I had."

"It blew over?"

"Not really very much time for that, was there?"

Morse sat and looked once more at this very ordinary woman he had come to visit, and his mind drifted back to Molly Bloom in *Ulysses*, and he knew that Mrs. Gilbert, too, was a woman who had offered, once, a presence and a bosom and a rose.

"Please tell me about this other woman."

"I don't know her real name—they call her 'Yvonne' at the clubs. But I know her initials—W.S.—and I know where she lives—23A Colebourne Road, just south of Richmond Road. It's only about five minutes' walk from the tube-station. . . ."

"You went to *see* her?"

"You don't know much about women, do you?"

"No, perhaps not," agreed Morse. But he was impatient now. He felt like a man with an enormously distended bladder who has been kept talking on the phone for half an hour, and he walked across to the door. "Will you be all right, Mrs. Gilbert?"

"Don't worry about me, inspector. I'll give the GP a ring when you've gone, and he'll give me a few tablets. They should take care of me for a little while, shouldn't they?"

"Yes, I'm sure they will. I know how you must be feeling—"

"Of course you don't! You've not the faintest idea. It's not today—it's not tonight. It's *tomorrow*. Can't you see that? You tell me Albert's dead, and in an odd sort of way it doesn't register. It's a shock, isn't it? And I'd be more than happy to live through one shock after another, but. . . ."

The tears were running freely again, and suddenly she moved towards him and buried her head on his shoulder. And Morse stood there by the door, awkward and inept; and (in his own strange way) almost loving the woman who was weeping out her heart against him.

It was several minutes before he was able to disengage himself and finally to stand upon the threshold of the opened door.

"Please look after yourself, Mrs. Gilbert."

"I will. Don't worry about that."

"If there's anything I can do to help. . . ."

She almost smiled. "Be gentle with the girl, inspector. You see, I know you're anxious to get away from here and see her, and I just want you to know that she's the loveliest girl—woman—I've ever met in all my life—that's all."

Tears were spurting again now, and Morse leaned forward and kissed her lightly on the forehead, in the sure knowledge that this woman had somewhere touched his feelings deeply. And as he walked slowly away up the road towards Manor House tube-station he doubted whether Albert Gilbert had ever really known the woman he had asked to marry him.

For all his conviction that the tide was running fully in his favour, the open doors of the Manor Hotel proved irresistible, and Morse wondered as he drained his pints and watched the pimps and prostitutes walk by whether, in a life so full of strange coincidence, he might at last be facing the wildest and most wonderful coincidence of them all: "W.S."! Browne-Smith had mentioned those initials . . . and Emily Gilbert had just repeated them . . . and those were the selfsame glorious initials of a girl whom once he'd known, and loved too well.

Twenty minutes after Morse had left the seventh floor of Berrywood Court, a key was inserted into the outer door of the Gilberts' flat, and a man walked in and flung his jacket carelessly down upon the sofa.

Two minutes later, Albert Gilbert, of Removals Anywhere, was talking (somewhat incoherently) over the phone to his GP, explaining how, for no apparent reason, his wife had fainted quite away on his return, and desperately demanding some instructions, since even now she showed no signs of sense or sanity returning.

CHAPTER
TWENTY-NINE

Tuesday, 29th July

> *All men, even those of a pessimistic nature, fall
> victim at certain points in their lives to the most
> extravagant of hopes.*

As Mrs. Gilbert had told him, Colebourne Road was
no more than five minutes' walk from East Putney tube-
station. But Morse appeared in no hurry, and when he
reached the streetsign he stopped awhile and stood beneath
it, deep in thought. Surely he couldn't be so utterly and
stupidly sentimental as to harbour even the faintest hope
that he was just about to see once more the woman whom
he'd worshipped all those years ago. No, he told himself, he
couldn't. And yet a wild, improbable hope lived on; and as
if to nourish the hope, he entered the Richmond Arms on
the corner of the street and ordered a double-Scotch. As he
drank, his thoughts went back to the time when he'd visited
his old mother in the Midlands, and gone off to an evening
Methodist service to see if a girl, a very precious girl, was
still in her place in the choir-stalls, still raising her eyes to
his at the end of each verse of every hymn and smiling at
him sweetly, and seraphically. But she hadn't been there—
hadn't been there for thirty years, perhaps—and he'd sat
by a pillar alone that night. Morse walked to the bar ("Same
again, please—Bell's"), and the name of Wendy Spencer
tripped trochaically across his brain. . . . It couldn't be the
same woman, though. It *wasn't* the same woman. And yet,
ye gods—if gods ye be—please make it her!

162

Morse's heart was beating at an alarming rate and his throat felt very dry as he rang the bell of Number 23. There was a light downstairs, a light upstairs; and the odds were very strongly on her being in.

"Yes?" The door was opened by a youngish, dark-complexioned woman.

"I'm a police inspector, Miss—"

"Mrs.—Mrs. Price."

"Ah yes—well, I'm looking for someone I think lives here. I'm not quite sure of her name but—"

"I can't help you much then, can I?"

"I think she's sometimes called 'Yvonne.'"

"There's no one here by that name."

The door had already closed an inch or two, but now there was another voice. "Anything *I* can do to help?"

A taller woman was standing behind Mrs. Price, a woman in a white bathrobe, a woman with freshly-showered and almost shining skin, a woman awkwardly re-making the tumbled beauty of her hair.

"He says he's a police inspector—says he's looking for someone called 'Yvonne,'" explained an aggressive Mrs. Price.

"Do you know her surname, inspector?"

Morse looked at the white-clad woman who now had moved towards the centre of the doorway, and a crushing wave of disappointment broke over him. "Not yet, I'm afraid. But I know she lives here—or she was shtaying—staying here until very recently."

"Well you must have got it wrong—" began Mrs. Price.

But the woman in white was interrupting her: "Leave this to me, Angela—it's all right. I think I may be able to help you, inspector. Won't you come in?"

Morse climbed the narrow stairs, noting the slim ankles of the woman who preceded him.

"Would you like a drink?" she asked, as they sat opposite each other in the small but beautifully furnished living-room.

"Er—no. Perhaps not."

"You've had enough already, you mean?"

"Does it show?"

She nodded—a faint smile upon lips that were thin and completely devoid of make-up. "It's the 's's that are always difficult, isn't it? When you've had too much drink, I mean—or when you begin wearing false teeth."

Morse looked at her own, most beautifully healthy teeth. "How would you know about that?"

"I sometimes drink too much."

Morse let it go, for things were going very nicely—the conversation moving already on to a plane of easy familiarity. But it wasn't to last.

"What do you want, inspector?" A hard, no-nonsense tone had come into her voice.

So Morse told her; and she listened in silence, occasionally crossing one naked leg over the other and then covering her knees with a sharp little tug at the robe, like some puritanical parson's wife at a vicarage tea-party. And almost from the start Morse felt the virtual certainty that 'Yvonne' had now been found—found sitting here in front of him, her head slightly to one side, sweeping up her blonde hair with her left hand and reinserting a few of the multitudinous pins with her right.

When Morse had finished the first part of his tale, she reached for her handbag. "Do you smoke, inspector?"

Morse patted his jacket pocket, and suspected that he must have left his own recently-purchased packet in the pub.

"Here, have one of these." Her bag was open now, the flap towards him; and seeing the faded gilt initials Morse knew that his silly hope was finally extinguished.

"You're very kind," he heard himself say.

Had she seen something vulnerable in this strange inspector of police? In his mien? In his eyes? On his lips? Perhaps, indeed, she had, for her voice had been more gentle, and she now stood up and lit his cigarette, unconscious (or uncaring) that her robe was partly open at the top as she leaned towards him. Then she sat back in her chair again, and told him her own side of the story, still occasionally recrossing her lovely legs, but now no longer too concerned about concealing them.

She'd known Bert Gilbert for only a few weeks. He'd come into the sauna one morning—very much in control of himself—and asked her if she'd be willing to entertain a very special client of his; yes, at the address Morse had mentioned; and, yes, with a sequel much as he'd described it. After that Gilbert had obviously taken a liking to her, spent a fair amount of money on her, and wanted to keep seeing her. *Had* kept seeing her. But he'd got jealous and morose, and was soon telling her that he wanted her to pack up her job and go to live with him. For her part, the whole thing had been the old familiar story of an ageing man behaving like an infatuated schoolboy—and she'd told him so.

That was all.

"What's your name?" asked Morse.

Her eyes were looking down at the thickly-piled carpet: "Winifred—Winifred Stewart. Not much of a name, is it? Some people are christened with horrid names."

"Mm."

She looked up. "What's your name?"

"They call me Morse: Inspector Morse."

"But that's your *surname*."

"Yes."

"You don't want to tell me your Christian name?"

"No."

"Like that, is it?" (She was smiling.)

Morse nodded.

"What about that drink? You've sobered up a bit, you know."

But (quite amazingly) Morse had hardly heard her. "Do you—do you go with lots of men?"

"Not lots, no. I'm a very expensive item."

"You earn a lot of money?"

"More than you do." Her voice had grown harsh again, and Morse felt sad and dejected.

"Do you get much pleasure from—er—"

"From having sex with clients? Not much, no. Occasionally though—if you want me to be honest."

"I'm not sure I do," said Morse.

She stood up and poured herself a glass of dry Vermouth, without renewing her offer to the Chief Inspector. "You don't know much about life, do you?"

"Not much, no." He seemed to her to look so lost and tired now, and she guessed he must have had a busy day. But had she known it, his mind was working at a furious rate. There was *something* (he knew it!) that he'd been missing all the way along; something he doubted he would learn from this disturbingly attractive woman; something that she probably couldn't tell him, anyway, even when she came (as he knew she would) to the second part of the tale she had to tell.

"When did you last see Gilbert?" he asked.

"I'm not sure—"

"You say you saw him quite a few times after you entertained his special client?"

It was puzzling to Morse how the tone of her voice could vary so vastly (and so suddenly) between the gentle and jarring. It was the latter again now.

"You mean did I go to bed with him?"

Morse nodded. And for the first time she was aware of the cold, almost merciless eyes that stared upon her, and she felt the sensation of a psychological and almost physical stripping as she answered him, her top lip quivering. "Yes!"

"Was that after you'd met your *second* special client?"

Her startled eyes looked into his, and then down to the Wilton again. "Yes," she whispered.

"Please tell me all about that," said Morse quietly.

For a few moments she said nothing; then she picked up her glass and quickly drained it.

"Before I do—would you like to come to bed with me?"

"No."

"Are you sure?" She stood up and loosened her belt, allowing the sides of her bathrobe to fall apart before drawing them together again and retying the belt tightly around her waist.

"Quite sure," lied Morse.

So Winifred Stewart (it was now past eight o'clock) told Morse about her second special client, a Mr. Westerby, who also hailed from Oxford. And Morse listened very carefully, nodding at intervals and seemingly satisfied. But he *wasn't* satisfied. It was all interesting—of course it was; but it merely corroborated what he'd already known, or guessed.

"What about that drink?" he asked.

Mrs. Angela Price looked knowingly at her husband when she finally heard the quiet voices on the doorstep. It was a quarter to midnight, and BBC 1 had already finished its transmission.

Lewis had finally gone to bed abut ten minutes before Morse found a taxi on the Richmond Road. He'd hoped that Morse would have been back before now, and had tried repeatedly to get in touch with him, both at HQ and at his home. For he had received a remarkable piece of news that same afternoon from the young porter at Lonsdale, who had received a card by second post; a card from Greece; a card from Mr. Westerby.

At 2 a.m., Winifred Stewart was still lying awake. The night was sultry and she wore no nightdress as she lay upon her bed, covered only by a lightweight sheet. She thought of Morse, and she felt inexpressibly glad that she had met him; longed, too, with one half of her mind, that he would come to visit her again. And yet she knew, quite certainly, that if he did her soul would be completely bared and she would tell him all she knew. Two thirds of the tragic tale had now been told; and if ever he began to guess the final truth. . . . Yet, with the other half of her mind she didn't want him back—ever—for she was now a very frightened woman.

At 3 a.m. she went to the bathroom to take some Disprin tablets.

At 4 a.m. she was still awake, and suddenly she felt the night had grown so very cold.

CHAPTER
THIRTY

Wednesday, 30th July

In which "The Religion of the Second Mile" is fully explained, and Morse is peremptorily summoned to his superior.

As he sat back comfortably in a first-class compartment of the 10 a.m. "125" from Paddington, Morse felt the residual glow of a great elation. For now (as he knew) the veil of the temple had been rent in twain.

The previous night he had missed the last train to Oxford and only just managed to find, on the highest floor of a cheap hotel, a cramped and claustrophobic room in which the water-pipes had groaned and gurgled through the early hours. But it was in this selfsame mean and miserable room that Morse, as he lay on his back in the darkness with both hands behind his head, had finally seen the amazing light of truth. Half occupied with the lovely woman he had left so recently, half with the older problems that beset him still, his mind had steadfastly refused to rest. He sensed that he was *almost* there, and the facts of the case raced round and round his brain like an ever-accelerating whirligig. The old facts . . . and the new facts.

Not that he had learned much that was surprisingly new from Mrs. Emily Gilbert. Nor, for that matter, from Miss Winifred Stewart—except for the confirmation that she had, indeed, agreed to entertain a second special guest from Oxford whose name was Mr. Westerby. There had been a few other things, though. She'd told him, for example, that Emily had been simultaneously wooed by each of the Gilbert brothers; that, of the two, Alfred was considerably the more interesting and cultured—particularly because of his love of music; but that it was Albert who had won the prize with his livelier, albeit coarser, ways. The brothers were still very much alike (she'd told him)—extraordinarily so in appearance—but if they'd been holidaying together in Salzburg Alfred would have gone to a Mozart concert and Albert to *The Sound of Music*. . . . Yes, that was something new; but it hardly seemed to Morse of much importance. Far more important was what she *hadn't* told him, for he had sensed the deep unease within her when she'd told him of her time with Westerby: not the unease of a woman telling obvious untruths; the unease, rather, of a woman telling something less than all she knew. . . .

It was at that very point in his whirling thoughts that Morse had jerked himself up in his bed, switched on the bedside lamp, and reached for the only object of comfort that the sombre room could offer him: the Gideon Bible that rested there beside the lamp. In two minutes his fumbling and excited fingers had found what he was seeking. There it was—St. Matthew, Chapter Five, Verse Forty-One: "And whosoever shall compel thee to go a mile, go with him twain." He remembered vividly from his youth a sermon on that very text—from a wild, Welsh minister: "The Religion of the Second Mile." And it was with the forty-watt bulb shedding its feeble light over the Gideon Bible that Morse smiled to himself in unspeakable joy, like one who has travelled on a longer journey still—that third and final mile. . . .

At last he knew the truth.

"In two minutes we shall be arriving at Oxford station," came the voice over the microphone. "Passengers for Banbury, Birmingham, Charlbury. . . ." Morse looked at his watch: 10:41 a.m. No need for any great rush now—no need for any rush at all.

He walked from the station up to the bus-stop in Cornmarket; and at 11:30 was back at Police HQ in Kidlington, where a relieved-looking Lewis awaited him.

"Good time, sir?"

"Marvellous!" said Morse, seating himself in the black leather chair and beaming benignly.

"We expected you back yesterday."

"'We?' Who's that supposed to mean?"

"The super was after your blood last night, sir—_and_ this morning."

"Ah, I see."

"I said you'd ring him as soon as you got in."

Morse dialled Strange's number immediately. Engaged.

"How about you, Lewis? You have a good time?"

"I don't know, sir. There's _this_."

He handed over the postcard he had picked up the previous evening from Lonsdale, and Morse looked down at a glossy photograph of ancient stones. He turned the card over, and read that such crumbling masonry was nothing less than the remains of the royal palace of Philip II of Macedon (382-336 BC). Then he saw the large Hellas stamp, featuring sea shells set against a blue-green background; then the message, neatly penned and very brief: "Wonderful weather. Any mail to Cambridge Way. Staying on a further week. Regards to the Master—and to your good selves. G.W."

"Lovely place, Greece, Lewis."

"I wouldn't know, I'm afraid."

"Perhaps Westerby doesn't know either," said Morse slowly.

"Pardon, sir?"

"You'd better keep it, of course—but he's not in Greece. It's a forgery—you can see that, surely!"

"But—"

"Look, Lewis! Look at that franking."

Lewis looked closely but saw little more than a blackened circle, with whatever lettering there may have been so smudged that it was quite illegible. He could, though, just about decipher one or two of the letters: there was an "O" (certainly) and an "N" (possibly) near the beginning of one word, and the next word probably ended in an "E." But he could make nothing of it, and looked up to find that Morse was smiling still.

"I shouldn't take too much notice of it, Lewis. It's not too difficult to get hold of a Greek postage-stamp, is it? And then if you get a date-stamp and push it vaguely one way instead of banging it straight down you'll get the same sort of blur as that. You see, someone just brought the card into the Lodge and left it handily upon a pile of mail. It's all a fake! And, if you like, I'll tell you where the date-stamp comes from: it comes from *Lonsdale College.*"

The phone rang before Lewis could make any answer, and a harsh voice barked across the line: "That you, Morse? Get over here—and get over here quick!"

"I think you're in the dog-house," said Lewis quietly.

But Morse appeared completely unconcerned as he rose to his feet and put his jacket on.

"I'll tell you something else about that card, Lewis. We know a man, don't we, who's been writing a book about our Mister Philip Two of Macedon—remember?"

Yes, Lewis did remember. Just as Morse had done, he'd seen the typescript on the desk in Browne-Smith's room, as well as the pile of postcards that had lain beside it. And, as Morse walked across to the door, he felt annoyed and disappointed with himself. There was one thing Morse hadn't mentioned, though.

"Is the handwriting a fake as well, sir?"

"I haven't the faintest idea," replied Morse. "Why don't you go and find out, if you can? No rush, though. I think the super and I may well be in for rather a longish session."

"Siddown, Morse!" growled Strange, his long gaunt face set grimly and angrily. "I heard last night—and again this morning—from the Metropolitan Commissioner." His eyes fixed Morse's as he continued. "It seems that a member of *my* force—*you*, Morse!—was witness to a major crime in London yesterday; that you left the scene of this crime without adequate explanation and in defiance of normal police procedures; that you allowed the only other witness of this crime to go off home—God!—a home incidentally which doesn't exist; that you then went off to see a woman up in North London to tell her that her husband had just been murdered; and if all that's not enough," the blood was rising in his face, "you couldn't even get the name of the bloody corpse right!"

Morse nodded agreement, but said nothing.

"You realize, don't you, that this is an extremely serious matter?" Strange's voice was quieter now. "It won't be in my hands, either."

"No, I understand that. And you're right, of course—it's a very serious matter. The only thing is, sir, I don't think that even you quite understand how desperately serious it is."

Strange had known Morse for many years and had marvelled many times at the exploits of this extraordinary and exasperating man. And there was something about the way in which Morse had just spoken that signalled a warning. It would be wise for him to listen, he knew that.

So he listened.

It was more than two hours later when Strange's middle-aged secretary saw the door open and the two men emerge. Earlier she had been informed that, short of a nuclear explosion, her boss was not to be disturbed; and she did know a little (how not?) of the reason for Morse's summons from on high. Yet now she saw that it was Strange's face which looked, of the two, the more drained and set; and she bent her head a little closer to the clattering keys, as if her presence there might cause embarrassment. The two men had said nothing more to each other, she was sure of that—except that Strange had murmured a muted "Thank you" as Morse had walked across the room. Then, after Morse was gone, and just before her boss had closed his office door, she thought she heard him speak once more: "My God!"

THE END OF THE SECOND MILE

THE THIRD MILE

CHAPTER THIRTY-ONE

Friday, 1st August

> *Like some latter-day Pilgrim, one of the pro-*
> *tagonists in this macabre case is determined to rid*
> *himself of his burden.*

Two days after the events described in the previous
chapter, a man looked about him with extreme circumspec-
tion before inserting one of his keys into the door at the rear
entrance of the luxury flats in Cambridge Way. The coast
was clear. Apart from the uniformed police constable standing outside the front entrance, he guessed (and guessed cor-
rectly) that at last he was alone. He moved silently up the
carpeted staircase and let himself into the room that faced
the first landing; there was just one thing he had to do.
Once inside the flat he fixed his rather ancient hearing-aid
into his right ear (exactly as he'd done three days before),
flicked over the lock on the Yale (a precaution he'd earlier
omitted to take), and took from his pocket a newly-pur-
chased screwdriver—a larger, shinier, more effective instrument than the one which had bored its way through
Gilbert's spine. He'd known the truth, of course, on that
previous visit; known it immediately he'd entered the main
sitting-room. For, although the crates seemed all (quite
properly) still unopened, from the mantelpiece Mercator's
head had stared at him accusingly. . . .

After performing his grisly task—it took him only a few
minutes—he retraced his steps to the rear entrance and let
himself out into the bright afternoon sunlight, where he

promptly hailed a taxi. He saw the driver's eyes flick to the mirror as his hearing-aid began to oscillate; so he turned off the volume and took it out. It had served its purpose well today, and he put it away and sought to relax as the taxi threaded its way through the heavy traffic. But his mind could give him little rest. . . . If only on that terrifying day. . . . But no! Awaiting Gilbert had been an almost certain early retribution. Money! That was all that Gilbert had demanded—then more money. An odd compulsion (as it appeared to the man in the taxi); certainly when compared with the motivations that dominated his own life—the harbouring of inveterate hatreds, and the almost manic ambition, sometimes so carefully concealed, for some degree of worldly fame.

"Here we are, sir: Paddington."

Why Paddington? Why not Euston, or Victoria, or Liverpool Street? Why *any* railway station? Perhaps it was the anonymity of such a place—a place at which he could deposit the burden of his sin that lay so heavily in the supermarket carrier-bag he tightly clutched as he walked through the swing doors of the Station Hotel and turned right to the gentlemen's toilet. No one else was there, and he closed the door behind him in the furthest of the cubicles that faced the open pissoir. Here, he lifted the plastic ring of the lavatory seat, climbed on to the circular fixture and lifted the covering of the porcelain cistern. But the water-filled cavity was far too narrow—and suddenly he was jerked into a frozen stillness, for he heard the door-catch click in a nearby cubicle. Something had to be done quickly. He felt inside the carrier-bag and took out a flat package wrapped round with a copy of *The Times*—a package which, judging from its shape, might have held two sandwiches, and which now plopped into the water and sank immediately to the bottom of the cistern.

Still carrying the bulk of his burden, he walked out of the hotel into the main-line station, where he drifted aimlessly about until he saw the planks and scaffolding at the furthest end of Platform One. He made his way slowly along this platform, intermittently turning his eyes upwards to take in Brunel's magnificent wrought-iron roof that arched above him. He had already seen the skip—half-full of building rubble and general rubbish. . . . Apart from a solitary orange-coated workman a few yards up the line, he was alone. Suddenly turning, he dropped his bag into the skip and sauntered back towards the unmanned ticket-barrier. He would have enjoyed a pot of searing hot tea and a buttered scone in the cool lounge of the Station Hotel, but he dared not trust himself. He was shaking visibly and the sweat was cold upon his forehead. It was time to return to base, to lie down awhile, to tell himself that the task he'd so much dreaded was now accomplished—if not accomplished well.

Crossing over Praed Street, he walked down to the bottom of Spring Street and entered a small hotel just off to the left. No one was on duty at the reception-desk, and he lifted the hinged board, took his key (Number 16) off its wall-hook, and climbed the stairs. Although he had now been in the same hotel for many days, he still felt some hesitation about which way up the key went in; and again, now, he fiddled and scraped a bit before opening the door and admitting himself to the small but neatly-furnished room. He took off his jacket, placed it at the bottom of the single bed, wiped his forehead with a clean white handkerchief from the antique wardrobe—and experienced a vast relief at finding himself safely back in this temporary home. The Gideon Bible, in its plum-coloured boards, still lay on the table beside the pillow; the window, as he had left it, was still half-open, providing easy access (he was glad of it!) to the fire-escape that zigzagged down the narrow side of the hotel to the mean-looking courtyard below. Turning round, he saw that the door to the wash-room was open, too, and he promised himself (but in a little while) a cool and guilt-effacing shower.

For the moment he lay down on top of the coverlet, with that curious amalgam of elation that springs from defiance of danger and knowledge of accomplishment. As a boy, he'd known it when climbing Snowdon with a Scout troup: for all the other boys, the route alongside one precipitous face had seemed a commonplace occurrence—yet for himself a source of great and secret pride. . . . It was strange that he should only have experienced that marvellous elation again so very late in life, and then so often in such a short period of time. . . . He closed his eyes, and almost moved his mind towards some neutral gear, untroubled, disengaged. . . .

But only a minute later his body was jarred into panic-stricken dread. Someone was standing over him; someone who said "Good afternoon"—and nothing more.

"You! *You!*"

His eyeballs bulged in fear and incredulous surprise, and if either of these emotions could be said to have been in the ascendant, perhaps it was that of surprise. But even as he cowered upon the coverlet, the packing twine was cutting deep into his neck; and soon his frantic spluttering and croaking grew quieter and quieter—until it was completely stilled. So died George Westerby, late Scholar and Senior Fellow of Lonsdale College in the University of Oxford.

CHAPTER THIRTY-TWO

Saturday, 2nd August

It is a characteristic of the British people that they complain about their railways. In this case, however, there appears little justification for such complaint.

It was 9:50 a.m. the following morning when the winsome receptionist looked up from her desk and took the room-key.

"Nice morning again, Mr. Smith?"

He nodded and smiled—that distinctively lop-sided smile of his. Since he'd been there, she'd almost always been on duty in the mornings; often, too, in the evenings, when she'd taken his order for an early-morning pot of tea—and also for *The Times*.

"I've got to leave this morning; so if you'll make out my bill, please?"

He sat down in one of the armchairs just opposite the reception desk, and breathed in very deeply. He'd spent another deeply troubled night, fitfully falling into semi-slumber, then waking up to find his blue pyjamas soaked in chilling sweat. Throughout these hours his head had thumped away as though some alien fiend were hammering inside his skull; and it was only after early tea that finally he'd slept a little while. He awoke just after 9 a.m., his head still aching, yet now with a dulled and tolerable pain. For a few minutes he had lain there almost happily, upon the creased and tumbled pillow. But soon the same old host of thoughts was streaming through the portals of his brain, his eyeballs rolling round beneath the shuttered lids. And one thought fought a leading way through all the crowd—and one decision was made.

"Mr. Smith? Mr. *Smith*?"

He heard her, and rose to pay the bill. Sometimes (as well he knew) his brain could play him false; but this particular contingency he had anticipated, and he paid his dues with ready cash, in notes of high denomination.

He left the Station Hotel (as Westerby had done before him) and walked to the ticket-office. Then, for many minutes, he stood in front of the high departures-board. But he could read nothing. His eyes no sooner focused on the times of trains for Oxford than the letters (white) upon their background (black) had leap-frogged astigmatically across his retina, leaving him in dizzied indecision.

He stepped to the nearest ticket-barrier.

"Can you tell me my best bet for Oxford, please?"

"Platform 9. Half-past ten. But you'll have to—"

"Thank you."

The train was already in the platform and he pulled himself up into an empty first-class compartment, putting his ticket carefully into his wallet and leaning back against the head-rest. . . .

Half an hour later he jerked forward as the train halted with something less than silken braking-power, and he looked out of the window: Reading. Still the solitary occupant of the compartment, he leant back again and closed his wearied eyes. Not long . . . and he'd be there!

Thirty-five minutes later he was jerked to a second awakening.

"Tickets, please!"

He was gratified that he could find his ticket so easily, but his head was throbbing wildly.

"This your ticket, sir?"

"Yes. Why?"

"I'm afraid you've missed your connection. We've just gone past Didcot. You're on your way to Swindon."

"What? I don't understand—"

"You should have changed at Didcot for the Oxford train. You must have nodded off."

"But I've got to get to Oxford. I've—I've just *got* to get there."

"Nothing we can do, sir. You'll have to get the next train back from Swindon—"

"But it's urgent!"

"As I say, you'll just have to wait till we get to Swindon." The collector punched the ticket and handed it back. "We won't worry about any excess fare, sir. Genuine mistake, I'm sure."

The next few minutes registered themselves in his mind as an aeon of frenzied agony. Sitting forward in his seat, he bit deep into the nails of his little fingers, fighting with all his powers to keep control of a brain that stood unsurely on a precipice.

Then the train stopped—more gently this time.

He was glad to find his legs steady as he got to his feet, and he felt much calmer now. He put the sweat-soaked handkerchief away inside his trouser-pocket, took his case from the luggage-rack, opened the left-hand door of the carriage—and stepped down into nothing. He fell on to the sharp tones of a slight embankment on the south side of the line, and lay there hurt and wholly puzzled. Yet, strangely, he felt profoundly comfortable there: it seemed so easy now to sleep. The sun was blazing down from the clear-blue sky, and his head—at last!—was free from pain.

"You all right, sir?"

The ticket-collector was crouching beside him, and he heard some faintly-sounding voices from afar.

"I'm sorry . . . I'm sorry. . . ."

"Let me just help you up, sir. You'll be all right."

"No! Please don't bother. I'm just sorry, that's all. . . ."

He closed his eyes. But the sun was blazing still beneath his eyelids, glowing like some fiery orange, whirring and—ever larger—spinning down towards him.

But still there was no pain.

"I'll go and get some help, sir. Shan't be a minute."

The ticket-collector vaulted nimbly up the shallow embankment, but already it was too late.

"Before you do that, please do one thing for me. I want to get a message to a Chief Inspector Morse—at the Thames Valley Police Headquarters. Please tell him I was— I was on my way to see him. Please tell him that *I* did it— do you understand me? Please tell him . . . that. . . ."

But the man beside the track was speaking to himself; and even the curious heads that poked through nearby carriage-windows could make no sense of all the mumbled words.

Suddenly the sun exploded in a yellow flash and a jagged, agonizing pain careered across his skull. With a supreme effort of will he opened his eyes once more; but all was dark now, and the sweat was pouring down his face and seeping inside his gaping mouth. He *had* a handkerchief, he knew: it was in his trouser-pocket. But he wanted a clean one. Yes, he had plenty of clean ones. Why, he'd only bought a box of Irish-linen ones so very recently . . . from the shop in the Turl . . . only a hundred yards away from Lonsdale College. . . .

Another man now knelt beside the body—a young neurosurgeon who was travelling up to Swindon General Hospital. But he could do nothing; and after a little while he looked up at the ticket-collector—then slowly shook his head.

CHAPTER
THIRTY-THREE

Saturday, 2nd August

Whose was the body found in the Thrupp canal? It becomes increasingly clear now that there are very few contenders remaining.

In recent years Lewis had seldom spent two nights away from Oxford, and he didn't care much for London. But it had been a busy and a fruitful time.

Late the previous Wednesday afternoon, Morse had insisted that it was to be he, Lewis, who should drive up the next morning. There was much to do (Morse had said): many loose ends to tie up; statements to be taken; and, not least, some needful explanations to be made. So Lewis had taken his instructions, had performed them more than adequately, and now (indulging his one real weakness in life) was driving far too fast along the M40 back to Oxford. It was mid-morning.

His London colleagues had been a friendly bunch, most of them speaking in a careless, aitchless Cockney— yet all of them shrewd and competent men. They could forgive Morse readily, of course, but none of them seemed to understand his actions very well. And Lewis, himself being only semi-enlightened, was unable to throw much further light. But certain things were now clear. The man found murdered in the top-storey flat in Cambridge Way was Alfred Gilbert, Esq., estate agent, and late bachelor of some parish or other in central London. The murder weapon (so plain for all to see!) had been the screwdriver so

183

conveniently found at the scene of the crime, upon whose handle were some smudgy prints that might or (as Lewis hoped) might not be soon identifiable. For the present there were few other clues. Of "Mr. Hoskins" the police could find no trace, nor expected to do so, since the residents of Cambridge Way had always had a woman as their part-time concierge. But the police had been mildly mollified when Lewis had been able to produce Morse's description of the man—from his age to his height, from chest-measurement to weight, from the colour of eyes to the size of his shoes.

After that, Lewis had done exactly as Morse had instructed. There had been three visits, three interviews, and three statements (slowly transcribed). First, the statement from the manager of the Flamenco Topless Bar; second, that from Miss Winifred Stewart, hostess at the Sauna Select; third, that from Mrs. Emily Gilbert at her home in Berrywood Court. All three, in their various ways, had seemed to Lewis to be nervously defensive, and more than once he had found himself seriously doubting whether any of the trio was over-anxious to come completely clean. But Morse had blandly told him that any further investigations were not only futile but also quite unnecessary; and so he had ignored some obvious evasions, and merely written down what each had been prepared to tell him.

Then, without much difficulty, he'd been able to discover at least something about the Gilbert brothers. Albert and the late Alfred had been public partners in a property-cum-removals firm, and private partners in a company christened Soho Enterprises—the latter owning, in addition to the topless bar, two dubious bookshops and a small (and strictly members-only) pornographic cinema. The London police knew a good deal about these activities anyway and enquiries were still proceeding, but already it seemed perfectly clear that even sex was suffering from the general recession. Of which fact Lewis himself was glad, for he found the Soho area crude and sordid; and had the tempter looked along those streets, he could have entertained only the most desperate hope of pushing that broad and solid back through any of the doorways there. Finally,

Lewis had been instructed to discover, if it were at all possible, the whereabouts of Albert Gilbert, Esq., although Morse had held out little prospect on that score—and Morse (as usual) had been right.

At the Headington roundabout Lewis was debating whether to call in for a few minutes and tell the missus he was safely home. But he didn't. He knew the chief would be waiting.

During the previous two days Morse had hardly over-exerted himself, fully recognizing his own incompetence in such matters as mounting a man-hunt or supervising the search (yes—yet another one!) of the waters out of Thrupp. But he *had* done two things, in each case retracing the ground that Lewis had trodden before him. First, he had visited the Blood Transfusion Centre at the Churchill Hospital, where he asked to look through the current records; where after only a couple of minutes he nodded briefly; where he then asked to see the records for the previous five years, in this second instance spending rather longer before nodding again, pushing the drawers of the filing-cabinet to, thanking the clerk, and departing. Second, he'd driven down to the Examination Schools, where he spent more than an hour with the Curator, finally thanking him, too, and leaving with the contented look of a man who has found what he sought. Now, again, as he sat at his desk that Saturday morning, he looked contented—and with even better reason, for the call had come through at 9:30. He'd *known* there must be something in the waters of the Thrupp canal. . . .

The sight of Lewis gladdened him even more. "Get some egg and chips while you were away?"

Lewis grinned. "Once or twice."

"Well, let's hear from you. By the way, I hope you've noticed: hardly any swelling at all now, is there?"

Twenty minutes later the phone rang.

"Morse here. Can I help you?"

Lewis observed that the Chief Inspector's pale, ill-shaven face was tautening as he listened. Listened only; till finally he said, "I'll be there as soon as I can," and with a look of unwonted agitation slowly put the receiver down.

"What was all that about, sir?"

"That was London on the line—Westerby's just been found—he's been murdered—they found him this morning—in a bedroom near Paddington—strangled with packing-twine."

It was Lewis's turn now to reflect with puzzlement on this troublous news. From what Morse had told him earlier, the case was almost over—with just a few arrests to come. So what on earth did *this* mean? But already Morse was on his feet and looking in his wallet.

"Look, Lewis! You just get those reports of yours sorted out and typed up—then get off home and see the missus. Nothing more for you today."

"You sure there's nothing I can do?"

"Not got a couple of fivers to spare, have you?"

After Morse had left, Lewis rang his wife to say that he'd be in for a latish lunch. Then, beginning to get his documents in order, he reached for *Chambers's Dictionary*: Morse was a fanatic about spelling.

The phone rang ten minutes later: it was the police surgeon.

"Not there? Where the 'ell's he got to, then?"

"One or two complications in the case, I'm afraid."

"Well, just tell the old bugger, will you, that the leg he's found would make the height about 5 foot 10 inches—5 foot 11 inches. All right? Doesn't help all that much, perhaps, but it might cut out a few of the little 'uns."

"*What* leg?" Lewis felt utterly confused.

"Didn't he tell you? Huh! Secretive sod, isn't he? He's had half a dozen divers out this last couple of days. . . . Still, he was right, I suppose. Lucky, though! Just tell him anyway—if he comes back."

"Perhaps he knew all the time," said Lewis quietly.

The phone was going all the time now. A woman's voice was put through from the operator: but, no, she would speak to no one but Morse. Then Strange (himself, this time), who slammed down the receiver after learning that Morse had gone to London. Then another woman's voice—

one Lewis thought he almost recognized: but she, too, refused to deal with any underling. Finally, a call came through from Dickson, on reception; a call that caused Lewis to jolt in amazement.

"You *sure*?"

"Yep. Swindon police, it was. Said he was dead when the ambulance got there."

"But they're sure it's *him*?"

"That's what they said, sarge—sure as eggs is eggs." Lewis put down the phone. It would be impossible to contact Morse in transit: he never drove anything other than his privately-owned Lancia. Would Morse be surprised? He'd certainly *looked* surprised about an hour ago on learning of the death of Westerby. So what about this? What about Dickson's latest information? That the body just recovered from a shallow embankment on the Didcot-Swindon railway-line was certainly that of Oliver Browne-Smith, late fellow of Lonsdale College, Oxford.

About the time that Lewis received his last call that morning, Morse was turning left at Hanger Lane on to the North Circular. He'd still (he knew) a further half-hour's driving in front of him, and with a fairly clear road he drove in a manner that verged occasionally upon the dangerous. But already he was too late. It had been a quarter of an hour earlier that the ambulance had taken away the broken body that lay directly beneath a seventh-storey window in Berrywood Court, just along the Seven Sisters Road.

Later the same afternoon, a business executive, immaculately dressed in a pin-striped suit, walked into the farthest cubicle of the gentlemen's toilet at the Station Hotel, Paddington. When he pulled the chain, the cistern seemed to be working perfectly, as though the presence of a pair of human hands as yet was causing little problem to the flushing mechanism.

CHAPTER
THIRTY-FOUR

Monday, 4th August

*In which Morse and Lewis retrace their journey
as far as the terminus of the first milestone.*

It was with growing impatience that Lewis waited from
8:15 a.m. onwards. Morse had arrived back in Oxford late
the previous evening and had called in to see him, readily
accepting Mrs. Lewis's offer to cook him something, and
thereafter settling down to watch television with the joyous
dedication of a child. He had refused to answer Lewis's
questions, affirming only that the sun would almost certainly rise on the morrow, and that he would be in the office—early.

At 9 a.m. there was still no sign of him, and for the
umpteenth time Lewis found himself thinking about the astonishing fact that, of the four dubiously-associated and
oddly-assorted men who had played their parts in the case,
not *one* of them could now lay the slightest claim to be mistaken for the corpse that still lay in Max's deep-refrigeration
unit: Browne-Smith had died of a brain haemorrhage beside
a railway-track; Westerby had been strangled to death in a
cheap hotel near Paddington; Alfred Gilbert had been
found murdered in a room a couple of floors above Westerby's flat in Cambridge Way; and Albert Gilbert had
thrown himself from a seventh-storey window in Berrywood
Court. So the same old question still remained un-
answered, and the simple truth was that they were running
out of bodies.

But there *were* one or two items that Lewis had discovered for himself, and at 9:30 a.m. he browsed through his neatly-typed reports once more. He'd learned, for example—from the manager of the topless bar—that Browne-Smith seemed to have been unaccountably slow in identifying himself by the agreed words: "It's exactly twelve o'clock, I see." Then (after applying a good deal of pressure) he'd learned from the same source that the ciné equipment had definitely not been returned to the bar the next day; in fact, it had been nearer a week before any of the bar-clients could indulge their voyeuristic fantasies again. There was a third fact, too: that neither the manager nor any of his hostesses had previously set eyes upon the man with the brownish beard who had sat beside the bar that fateful Friday when Browne-Smith had been tempted down from Oxford. . . .

Morse finally arrived just before 9:45 a.m., his lower lip caked with blood.

"Sorry to be late. Just had her out. No trouble. Hardly felt a thing. 'Decayed beyond redemption'—that's what the little fellow said." He sat down expansively in his chair. "Well, where do you want me to start?"

"At the beginning, perhaps?"

"No. Let's start before then, and get a bit of the background clear. While you were off gallivanting in London, Lewis, I called in to see your pal at the Examination Schools, and I asked him just one thing: I asked him what he thought were the potential areas for any crooked dealings in this whole business of the final lists. And he made some interesting suggestions. First, of course, there's the possibility of someone getting results ahead of the proper time. Now this isn't perhaps one of the major sins; but, as you told me yourself, all that waiting can become a matter of great anxiety: sometimes perhaps *enough* anxiety to make one or two people willing to pay—pay in *some* way—for learning results early. That's only the start of it, though. You see if there's some undergraduate who's *nearly* up to the first-class honours bracket, he's put forward for a viva-voce examination, but he's never told which particular part of his work he's going to be re-examined in. Now, if he *did* know, he'd be able to swot up on that side of things and get ready to catch all the hand-grenades they lobbed at him. Agreed? But let's go on a stage further. Our budding 'first' would be an even shorter-odds favourite if he knew the *name* of the man who was going to viva him: he could soon find out this fellow's hobby-horses, read his books, and generally tune himself in to the right wavelength. Which leads on to the final consideration. If he did know exactly who it was who was going to settle his future, there'd always be the potential for a bit of *bribery*—the offer of money in return for that glowing recommendation for a 'first.' You see, Lewis? The whole process is full of loop-holes! I'm not saying anyone wriggles through 'em: I'm just telling you they're *there*. And, depending on what the rewards are, there might be a few susceptible dons who could feel tempted to go along with one or two suggestions, don't you think?"

Lewis nodded, "Perhaps a few might, I suppose."

"No 'perhaps,' Lewis—just a few *did*!"

Again Lewis nodded—rather sadly—and Morse continued.

"Then we found a corpse with a great big question-mark on the label round its neck."

"It hadn't got a neck, sir."

"That's true."

"And there isn't a question-mark any longer?"

"Patience, Lewis!"

"But we had the letter to go on."

"Even that, though. If we hadn't had a line on things to start with, the whole thing would have been a load of gobbledygook. Would *you* have made much of it without—"

"I wouldn't have made anything of it, anyway."

"Don't underestimate yourself, Lewis—let me do it for you!"

"What about the blood-donor business?"

"Ah! Now if you've been a donor for a good many years you get a lot of little tiny marks—"

"As a matter of fact I got my gold badge last year—for fifty times, that is—in case you didn't know."

"Oh!"

"So I don't really need you to tell me much about *that*."

"But you *do*. Do you know when you have to pack up giving blood? What age, I mean?"

"No."

"Well, you bloody should! Don't you read any of the literature? It's *sixty-five*."

Lewis let the information sink in. "You mean that Browne-Smith wouldn't have been on the current records. . . ."

"Nor Westerby. They were both over sixty-five."

"Ye-es. I should have looked in the old records."

"It's all right. I've already checked. Browne-Smith *was* a donor until a couple of years ago. Westerby never: he'd had jaundice and that put him out of court, as I'm sure you'll know!"

"But the body *wasn't* Browne-Smith's."

"No?" Morse smiled and wiped the blood gently from his mouth. "Whose was it then?"

But Lewis shook his head. "I'm just here to listen, sir."

"All right. Let's start at the beginning. George Westerby is just finishing his stint at Lonsdale. He's looking for a place in London, and he finds one, and buys it. The estate agent tells him that all the removals from Oxford can easily be arranged, and that suits Westerby fine. He's got two places: his rooms in Lonsdale, and his little weekend cottage out at Thrupp. So Removals Anywhere come on to the scene—and the supremely important moment in the case arrives: Bert Gilbert notices the name opposite Westerby's rooms on T staircase—the name of Dr. O. M. A. Browne-Smith—the name of a man he'd always ranked among the legion of the damned—the man who'd been responsible for his younger brother's death.

"Now, very soon after this point—I'm sure of it!—we get a switch of brothers. Bert reports his extraordinary finding to his brother, and it's Alfred—by general consent the abler of the two—who now takes over. He finds out as much as he can about Browne-Smith, and devises a plan that makes it ridiculously easy for Browne-Smith to go along

with things. He writes a letter on Westerby's typewriter—
he's in Westerby's rooms whenever he .likes now, remember—inviting Browne-Smith to do him a very small
favour, and one that would entail no real compromise to
Browne-Smith's academic integrity. This offer, as we know,
was taken up, and off Browne-Smith goes to London. But
we also know—because he told us—that Browne-Smith
played his own cards with equal cunning. And in the end
Gilbert's plan misfired—whatever that plan had been originally.

"Gilbert came into the room to find that Browne-Smith
wasn't unconscious, as he'd expected. So they talked together straightaway; and it wasn't long before Gilbert discovered that the military records of young brother John
were hardly a striking example of dedication to duty. In fact,
far from being killed in action, he'd shot himself the night
before El Alamein—and one of the few people who knew all
this was Browne-Smith, John Gilbert's platoon officer. So
when the whole story was out at last, there couldn't have
been much wind left in the Gilberts' sails, because it was
quite clear to them that Browne-Smith hadn't the slightest
responsibility, direct or indirect, for their brother's death!
Now, at that point everything could have been over, Lewis.
And if it had been, certainly four of the five people who've
died in this case would still be alive. But . . ."

Yes, Lewis understood all this. It seemed simpler,
though, now that Morse had put it into words. "But then,"
he said quietly, "Browne-Smith saw the chance to dupli-
cate—"

"'Replicate'—that's the word I'd use, Lewis."

"—to replicate the process with Westerby."

"That's it. That's the end of the first mile, and we're
soon going to start on the second."

"Off we go then, sir!"

"Do you fancy a cup of coffee?"

Lewis got to his feet. "Any sugar?"

"Just a little, perhaps. You know it's a funny thing.
There were no end of tins of coffee in Alfred Gilbert's flat,
and not a single drop of alcohol!"

"Not everybody drinks, sir."

"'Course they do! He was just an oddball—that's for certain. And I'll tell you something else. When I was a lad I heard of a Methodist minister who was a bit embarrassed about being seen reading the Bible all the time—you know, on trains and buses. So he had a special cover made—a sort of cowboy cover with a gun-slinger on his horse; and he had this stuck round his Bible when he was reading Ezekiel or something. Well, I found a book in Gilbert's flat that was exactly the opposite. It had a cover on it called *Know Your Köchel Numbers*—"

"Pardon, sir?"

"'Köchel.' He was the chap who put all Mozart's works into some sort of chronological order and gave 'em all numbers."

"Oh."

"I had a look in this book—and do you know what I found? It was a load of the lewdest pornography I've ever seen. I—er—I brought it with me, if you want to borrow it?"

"No, sir. You read it yourself. I—"

"I *have* read it." The numbed lips were smiling almost guiltily: "Read it twice, actually."

"Did you find anything else in the flat?"

"Found a beard—a brownish beard. Sort of theatrical thing, stuck with Elastoplast."

"That all?"

"Found a scarf, Lewis. Not quite so long as mine, but a nice scarf. Still, that was hardly a surprise, was it?"

"Just a little sugar, you say?"

"Well, perhaps a bit more than that."

Lewis stood at the door. "I wonder whether Gilbert had *his* tooth out."

"Didn't need to, Lewis. He had false teeth—top and bottom."

CHAPTER THIRTY-FIVE

Monday, 4th August

*Gently we journey along the second mile, which
appears to Morse to be adequately posted.*

During the few minutes that Lewis was away, Morse
was acutely conscious of the truth of the proposition that the
wider the circle of knowledge the greater the circumference
of ignorance. He was (he thought) like some tree-feller in
the midst of the deepest forest who has effected a clearing
large enough for his immediate purposes; but one, too, who
sees around him the widening ring of undiscovered
darkness wherein the wickedness of other men would never
wholly be revealed. On his recent visit to London he had
felled a few more trees; and doubtless he and Lewis (before
the case was closed) would fell a few more still. But the men
who might have directed his steps through the trackless forest were now all dead, leaving him with an odd collection of
ugly, jagged stumps; ugly, jagged, awkward clues that could
only tell a stark, truncated version of the truth. But that was
all he had and—almost—it was enough, perhaps.

"Tell me more about the Gilberts," said Lewis, handing across a paper cup of tepid coffee.

"Well, you know as much about their background as I
do. Just remember one thing, though. We learned they
were identical twins, so closely alike that even their friends
got them muddled up occasionally. But when you get to
your sixties, Lewis, you're bound to differ a bit: general
signs of ageing, spots on the chin, gaps in the teeth, hair-

style, scars, whether you're fatter or thinner, the way you dress—almost everything is going to mark some ever-widening difference as the years go by. Now, I never saw Bert Gilbert alive—and I didn't go and look at him when he was dead. You see, it was *Alfred* Gilbert I met in Westerby's rooms that day—with a scarf wrapped round the bottom half of his face and a phoney tale about an abscessed tooth."

"He was frightened Browne-Smith would recognize him."

"Not just that, though. As it happened, Browne-Smith had already recognized his brother—although Alfred Gilbert wasn't to know *that*. Like all visitors, Bert had already reported to the Porter's Lodge a couple of times, and Alfred was anxious that *no one* should know that he and his brother had switched roles. He carefully selected a young assistant who'd only just joined the firm and who wouldn't know and wouldn't care which brother did what anyway—"

"But why all the bother, sir? Seems so unnecessary."

"Ah! But you're missing the point. The plan they'd concocted demanded far more shrewdness—and, yes, far more *knowledge*—than poor Bert could ever have coped with. Just think! It involved a close knowledge of Browne-Smith's position and duties in the College—and in the University. It involved an equally close knowledge of how final examinations work, and all the complicated procedures of results and so on. It's not *easy* to find all that stuff out. Not unless—"

"Unless *what*, sir?"

"When I went to London I found out quite a lot about Alfred Gilbert. He *wasn't* a bachelor. In fact, he was divorced about ten years ago, and his ex-wife—"

"I suppose you went to see her."

"No. She's living in Salisbury—but I rang her up. They had one child, a son. Know what they christened him, Lewis?"

"John."

Morse nodded. "After the younger brother. He was a bright lad, it seems, won a place at Oxford to read Music, and got a very good 'second.' In fact," Morse continued with great deliberation, "he had viva for a 'first.'"

Lewis sat back in his chair. All the pieces seemed to be falling neatly into place—or almost all of them.

"Back to the main sequence of events, though. Browne-Smith went to London on Friday the 11th of July, and that doesn't leave much time before most of the class-lists are due to be posted up. So if he decides—as he does—that he's going to repeat the broad outlines of the plan, he's got to get a move on. The Gilbert brothers had to be in on it, too, of course, and no doubt Browne-Smith agrees to pay them handsomely. There's no time for any chancy postal delay, so Browne-Smith drafts a careful letter to Westerby, and that letter, too, was probably written on Westerby's typewriter the next day, Saturday the 12th, when Alfred Gilbert went up to Oxford again, and when Westerby was out clearing up his odds and ends at Thrupp. The letter—'By Hand' it must have been—was left on Westerby's desk, I should think—"

"How do you know all this?"

"I don't really. But what I know for sure is that Westerby turned up at an address in London at 2 p.m. on Tuesday the 15th."

"Not Cambridge Way, though, surely? That was his *own* address."

"No—but Alfred Gilbert wasn't short of a few vacant properties, was he? And in fact it wasn't all that far from Westerby's flat, a little place—"

"Yes, all right, sir. Go on!"

"Now we come to the most fateful moment in the case. Westerby was given the same treatment as Browne-Smith: same pattern all through, same woman, same bottles of booze, with a few drops of chloral hydrate or something slipped in. But Westerby's not so canny as Browne-Smith was, and very soon he's lying there dead to the world on a creaking bed. *But what exactly happened then?* That's the key to the case, Lewis. Messrs. W and S are waiting outside—"

"*Who*, sir?"

"They're in your statement, Lewis—the men who made the arrangements at the topless bar. Haven't you heard of W. S. Gilbert?"

"Yes, but—"

"You know what 'W. S.' stands for, don't you? William Schwenck!"

"Oh."

"You know, there's *something* to be said in the Gilberts' favour: at least they had a warped sense of humour. You remember the name Soho Enterprises is registered under?"

Lewis remembered: Sullivan! He shook his head and then nodded. He knew he wasn't being very bright.

"Anyway," continued Morse, "Browne-Smith and Westerby are left alone. And when Westerby gradually comes round—with a splitting headache, I should think— he finds his age-long antagonist sitting on the bed beside him. And they talk—and no doubt soon they have a blazing row . . . and please remember that Browne-Smith's got his old army revolver with him! And yet . . . and yet, Lewis. . . ."

"He doesn't use it," added Lewis in a very quiet voice.

"No. Instead they stay there talking together for a long, long time; and finally they bring one of the Gilbert Brothers in—and at that point the road is twisting again to take us forward on the third and final mile."

Morse finished his coffee, and held out the plastic cup. "I enjoyed that, Lewis. Little more sugar this time, perhaps?"

The phone rang whilst Lewis was gone. It was Max.

"Spending most of your time in Soho, I hear, Morse."

"I'll let you into a secret, Max. My sexual appetite grows stronger year by year. What about yours?"

"About that leg? Lewis tell you about it?"

"He did."

"Remember that piece you put in the paper? You got the colour of your socks wrong."

"What do you expect. I hadn't got a leg to *go* on, had I?"

"They were purple!"

"Nice colour—purple."

"With green-suede shoes?"

"You don't dress all that well yourself sometimes."

"You said they were blue!"

"Just sticking the blinker out in the middle of a blizzard."

"What? *What?*"

"I've not had your report yet."

"Will it help?"

"Probably."

"You know who it is?"

"Yes."

"Want to tell me?"

So Morse told him; and for once the humpbacked man was lost for words.

CHAPTER
THIRTY-SIX

Monday, 4th August

We near the end, with two miles and four furlongs
of the long and winding road now completed.

"We found the body," resumed Morse, "on Wednesday
the 23rd, and the odds are that it had been in the water
about three days. So the man must have been murdered
either the previous Saturday or Sunday."

"He could have been murdered a few days before that,
surely?"

"No chance. He was watching the telly on the Friday
night!"

Lewis let it go. If Morse was determined to mystify
him, so be it. He'd not interfere again unless he could help
it. But one plea he did make. "Why don't you simply tell
me what you think happened—even if you're not quite sure
about it here and there?"

"All right. A *third* man goes to London on Saturday the
19th, taking up an offer which nobody in this case seems
able to refuse. This time, though, all the initial palaver is
probably dispensed with, and there's no intermediary stop
at the topless bar. This third man is murdered—by Browne-
Smith. And if *both* the Gilberts were there, we've got four
men on the scene with a body on their hands—a body
they've got to get rid of. Of the four men, Westerby is wet-
ting his pants with panic; and after a few tentative arrangements are made with him, he goes off—not, as we know,
back to Oxford, but to a cheap hotel near Paddington. The

other three—I think that Bert had probably kept out of the
way while Westerby was still there—now confer about what
can and what must be done. The body can't just be dumped
anyhow and anywhere—for reasons that'll soon be clear,
Lewis. It's going to be necessary, it's agreed, to sever the
head, and to sever the hands. That gruesome task is performed, in London, by one of the Gilberts—I should think
by Bert, the cruder of the pair—who promises Browne-
Smith that the comparatively uncumbrous items he's just
detached can be disposed of safely and without difficulty.
Then two of the three, Browne-Smith and Bert Gilbert,
drive off to Oxford in Westerby's Metro—and with Westerby's prior consent. It's probably the only car immediately
available anyway; but it's got one incalculable asset, as you
know, Lewis.

"Once in Oxford—this is late Sunday evening now—
Browne-Smith lets himself into Lonsdale via the back door
in The High and goes into his rooms and takes one item
only—a suit. I'm pretty sure, by the way, that it must have
been on a second trip to his rooms, later—after Westerby
decided he'd little option but to cancel his Greek holiday—
that he took the Lonsdale College stamp and one of his
Macedonian postcards. Anyway, the two men drive out to
Thrupp—the only likely stretch of water either of 'em can
think of—where they stop, without any suspicion being
roused, in Westerby's car, outside Westerby's cottage, to
which Bert Gilbert has the key. Once inside with the body,
Gilbert is willing (what he was paid for all this we shall
never know!) to perform the final grisly task—of taking off
the dead man's clothes and re-dressing him in Browne-
Smith's suit. Then, long after the Boat Inn is closed, the two
men carry the body the hundred yards or so along to the
one point where no boats are moored or can be moored: the
bend in the canal by Aubrey's Bridge. The job's done. It
must have been in the early hours when the two of them get
back to London, where the faithless Bert returns to his
faithful Emily, and Browne-Smith to his room in the Station
Hotel at Paddington. All right so far?"

"Are you making some of it up, sir?"

"Of course I bloody am! But it fits the clues, doesn't it? And what the hell *else* can I do? They're all *dead*, these johnnies. I'm just using what we *know* to fill in what we *don't* know. You don't object, do you? I'm just *trying*, Lewis, to match up the facts with the psychology of the four men involved. What do *you* think happened?"

Morse always got cross (as Lewis knew) when he wasn't sure of himself, especially when "psychology" was involved—a subject Morse affected to despise; and Lewis regretted his interruption. But one thing worried him sorely: "Do you really think Browne-Smith would have had the belly for all that business?"

"He wasn't a congenial murderer, if that's what you mean. But the one real mystery in this case is that one man—Browne-Smith—actually did so many inexplicable things. And there's more to come! What we've got to do, Lewis, is not to explain behaviour but to consider *facts*. And there's a very sad but also a very simple *factual* explanation of all this, as you know. I rang up a fellow in the Medical Library to learn something about brain-tumours, and he was telling me about the completely irrational behaviour that can sometimas result. . . . Yes . . . I wonder just what Olive Mainwearing of Manchester actually *did*. . . ."

"Pardon, sir?"

"You see, Lewis, we're not worried about his belly— we're worried about his *mind*. Because he acted with such a weird combination of envy, cunning, remorse, and just plain *ambivalence*, that I can't begin to fathom his motives." Morse shook his head. "I'll tell you one thing, Lewis. I'm just beginning to realize what a fine thing it is to have a mind like mine that's mainly motivated by thoughts of booze and sex—infinitely healthier! But let's go on. Just one more point about the body. Murderers aren't usually quite as subtle as people think; and you were absolutely right, as you know, when you mentioned that pleasure-cruiser off the Bahamas or somewhere. In Max's first report he said the legs were sheared off far more neatly than the other bits—and it's now clear that a boat-propeller hit the body and lopped the legs off. Well done!"

Lewis remained silent, deciding not to raise the subject of the corpse's socks.

"Back to Browne-Smith. His actions that next week are even stranger in some ways. *Abyssus humanae conscientiae!*"

Again, even more praiseworthily, Lewis remained silent.

"On the Monday his conscience was crucifying him, and he writes me—*me*—a long letter. I just don't know why we had the devious delivery through the bank . . . unless he thought he'd be giving himself a few days' grace in which he could cancel his confession. Because that's what it was. But it was something else, too. If you read the letter carefully, it contains a much more subtle message: in spite of vilifying Westerby throughout, it completely and deliberately exonerates him! And make no mistake; it was certainly Browne-Smith himself who wrote that letter. I *knew* him, and no one else could have caught that dry, exact, pernickity style. It's almost as though with one half of his fevered brain he *wanted* us—wanted *me*, one of his old pupils—to find out the whole truth; and yet at the same time the other half of his brain was trying to stop us all the time with those messages and cards . . . I dunno, Lewis."

"I think the psychologists have a word for that sort of thing," ventured Lewis.

"Well we won't bother about that, will we!"

The phone rang in the ensuing silence.

"That's good. . . . Well done!" said Morse.

"Can you describe them a bit?" asked Morse.

"Yes, I thought so," said Morse.

"No. Not the nicest job in the world, I agree. It'll be all right if I send my sergeant?" asked Morse.

"Fine. Tomorrow, then. And I'm grateful to you for ringing. It'll put a sort of finishing touch to things," said Morse.

"Who was that, sir?"

"Do you know, there've been some thousands of occasions in my life when I've looked forward to a third pint of beer, but I can't ever recollect looking forward to a third cup of coffee before!"

He held out the plastic cup, and once more Lewis walked away.

CHAPTER THIRTY-SEVEN

Monday, 4th August

Morse almost completes his narrative of the main events—with a little help from his imaginative faculties.

Only recently had Morse encountered the use of the word "faction" in the sense of a combination of fact and fiction. Yet such a combination was all he could claim in any convincing reconstruction of the final events of the present case. While Lewis was away, therefore, he reminded himself of the few awkward facts remaining that had to be fitted somehow into the puzzle: the fact that he had been forcibly (significantly?) detained for an extra half-hour after his interrogation of the manager of the topless bar; that the door of Number 29, Cambridge Way had (for what reason?) been finally opened to him; that the head of Gerardus Mercator had been prominently (accusingly?) displayed on the mantelpiece of Westerby's living-room; that an affluent Arab, doubtless a resident in the property, had looked round at him with such puzzlement (and suspicion?); and that somehow (via Browne-Smith?) Bert Gilbert had discovered Westerby's address in London, and (via the fire-escape?) managed to enter Westerby's room. Thus it was that when Lewis returned Morse was ready with his eschatology.

"The manager of the Flamenco, Lewis, has a wife, called 'Racquel.' When I got there, he tipped her the wink that something was seriously askew, and she made an urgent phone-call to 'Mr. Sullivan'—alias Alfred Gilbert—

204

who in turn told her that whatever happened they'd got to keep me in the place for a while. Why? Clearly because there was something that had to be done quickly, something that *could* be done quickly, before I turned up in Cambridge Way. The Gilberts, you see, were already collecting their pickings from Browne-Smith, but not as yet from Westerby. And so to remind Westerby that *he* was still up to his neck in hot water, too, they'd decided on a most appropriate niche for a corpse's head—that space in one of Westerby's crates where another head had originally nestled. It was imperative, therefore, that one of the Gilberts—Alfred, as it turned out—should go and clear away the damning evidence waiting in Westerby's flat. But late that same morning Westerby himself decided that it was reasonably safe now for him to return to his flat, and the first thing he saw there was the head of Mercator on the mantelpiece, and he suspected the grim truth immediately. Which is more than I did, Lewis! When Alfred Gilbert let himself in, Westerby was probably just opening the fateful crate; and somehow Westerby killed him—"

"Sir! That's not good enough. *How* did he do it? And why should he *need* to do it? They were both accomplices, surely?"

Morse nodded. "Yes, they were. But just think a minute, Lewis, and try to picture things. Alfred Gilbert is in a frenetic rush to reach Cambridge Way. He doesn't know *why* the police have got on to Cambridge Way, but he does know what they'll find if they visit Westerby's flat. They'll find what he himself and his brother have left there, almost certainly with the intention of some future blackmail. And, as I say, that evidence has got to be removed with the utmost urgency. So he lets himself into the flat, never expecting to find Westerby there, and never, I suspect, actually seeing him anyway. Westerby's got his hearing-aid plugged in, although, as your own notes say, Lewis, he's only slightly deaf; and when he hears the scrape of the key in the lock, he beats a panic-stricken retreat into the bathroom, where he watches the intruder through the hinged gap of the partially open door.

"Now Westerby himself hasn't the faintest idea that the police are on their way, has he? What he *suspects*—what he's been strongly suspecting even before opening the crate—is that it's been Gilbert—who else?—who's mis-led him so wickedly. Instead of Gilbert getting rid of the murdered man's head, that same head is resting even now in one of his own crates! He's just found it! I think he sees in a flash how crude, how indescribably callous, his so-called accomplice has been. He sees something else, too, Lewis. He sees Gilbert walking straight over to the crate, and at that point he *knows* who it is who's been plotting to implicate him further—doubtless for even more money—in this tragic and increasingly hopeless mess. He feels in his soul a savage compulsion to rid himself of that fiend who's kneeling over the crate, and he creeps back into the room and with all the force he can muster he stabs his screwdriver between those shoulder-blades.

"Then? Well, I can only guess that Westerby must have dragged him into the bathroom, straightway: because while there were no blood-stains on the carpet, the bathroom floor had only just been cleaned. Yes, I saw that, Lewis!

"Next, using the bunch of keys he found in Gilbert's pocket, Westerby took the body up in the lift to the top-floor flat—a flat he knew was still vacant—a flat he'd probably looked over himself when he was deciding on his future home. He locked away the body in a cupboard there, then went down again, cleaned up his own flat in his apron, and heard—at last!—someone ringing the main doorbell—me!—and *answered* it. *Why*, Lewis? Surely that's utter folly for him! Unless—unless he'd previously arranged to *meet* someone in Cambridge Way. And the only man he'd have been anxious to meet at that point is the one man he'd been avoiding like the plague for the last five years of his life—Browne-Smith! But instead—he finds *me*! And he now gives the performance of his life—impersonating a concierge called 'Hoskins.' You knew, Lewis, he was a Londoner? Yes. It's in your admirable notes on the man. I ought to have seen through the deception earlier, though; certainly I ought to have read the signs more intelligently when one of the tenants turned around and stared so curiously at me. But it *wasn't* just me: he was staring at *two* strangers!

"During that same lunch-time there were other things afoot. Alfred Gilbert had left a message for his brother, and now it was Bert Gilbert who got round to Cambridge Way as quickly as he could. There—I'm almost sure of it—he met Browne-Smith; and Browne-Smith told Bert Gilbert that he'd seen *me* go in, admitted by Westerby. At that moment, Bert must have seen the emergency signals flashing at full beam. He had no key—Alfred had taken the bunch—either to the front door or the back; so the two of them agreed to split up, with Browne-Smith watching the front and Bert Gilbert the back. What happened then? Gilbert saw Westerby leave! So he went round to tell Browne-Smith; and both of them were very puzzled, and very frightened. *I* was still in there, and so was Alfred Gilbert! Probably it was at that point that Bert Gilbert got to know from Browne-Smith where Westerby was staying, because it's clear that later on he *did* know. For the moment, however, they observed from a discreet distance—only to find that I didn't come *out* before the police went *in*. So they knew something had gone terribly wrong. Later, of course, they both learned of the murder of Alfred Gilbert, and they both drew their own conclusion—the *same* conclusion.

"In the days that followed Gilbert must have watched and waited, because he knew that it would now be imperative for Westerby to return to the flat to find out, one way or the other, whether the police had discovered those objects hidden in a relidded crate—objects, Lewis, which must have been a cause of recurrent nightmares to him. When Westerby finally risked his expedition, Gilbert made no attempt to abort the mission, because it was just as valuable for himself as for Westerby. He followed his quarry back from the flat to Paddington—for all I know he might even have followed him into the gents where the London lads found the corpse's hands. By the way, Lewis, you'd better tell the missus you've got another trip tomorrow.

"But then Gilbert stopped tailing Westerby, and went along to that nearby hotel, where he found an easy access to

Westerby's room—either by the fire-escape or by the seldom-tenanted reception desk. But let's leave those details to our metropolitan colleagues, shall we? They're going to find one or two people who saw something, surely? It's not our job. After Westerby got back to his room? Well, I dunno. But I'd like to bet that Westerby almost jumped out of his wilting wits when he found himself confronted by the man he thought he'd killed! You see, I doubt if at any stage Westerby was aware that there *were* two Gilberts—even less that they were still extraordinarily alike in physical appearance. Whatever the truth of that may be, Westerby was strangled in his room, and the long and tragic sequence of events has almost run its Aeschylean course.

"Not quite though. Browne-Smith had now decided that things had gone far too far, and I vaguely suspect that he was on his way to see *me* last Saturday. At least, we've got the evidence of the ticket-collector that Browne-Smith had some very urgent business here in Oxford. Pity . . . but perhaps it was for the best, Lewis. Then, the same Saturday, Bert Gilbert went home and found—as the police found—a note from his wife, Emily, saying that she couldn't stand any more of it, and that she'd left him. And Bert Gilbert—without any doubt the bravest of the three brothers—now faced both the fear of discovery and the knowledge of failure. So he opened his seventh-floor window and he jumped. . . . Poor sod! Perhaps you think it's a bit out of character, Lewis, for Bert Gilbert to do something as cowardly as that? But it was in the family, if you remember. . . ."

During this account, Morse had forgotten his coffee and he now looked down with distaste at the dark brown skin that had formed on its surface.

"Are the pubs open yet?" he asked.

"As always, sir, I think you know the answers to your own questions better than I do."

"Well, they will be, I should think, by the time we get to Thrupp. Yes, we're going to have a quiet little drink together, my old friend, at the end of yet another case."

"But you haven't told me yet—"

"You're quite right. There's one big central jigsaw piece that's missing, isn't there?"

CHAPTER
THIRTY-EIGHT

Monday, 4th August

The Third Milestone

In normal circumstances, thought Lewis, Morse would have looked a good deal happier as he mumbled "Cheers" before burying his nose in the froth; but there was a sombre expression in the chief's face as he spoke quietly across a small table in the lounge-bar of the Boat Inn.

"If this case ever comes to court, Lewis, there'll be several crucial witnesses—but the most important of all of them will be the man who tries to tell the judge about the power of hatred that can spring from thwarted ambition; and there were two men in Lonsdale College who had exemplified that terrible hatred for many years.

"The particular reason for their hatred was an unusual one, perhaps—but also an extremely simple one. Each of them had failed to be elected to the Mastership of Lonsdale, the position they'd both craved. Now, as we found out, the College rules require a minimum of six of the eight votes available to be cast in favour of any candidate, and not a single vote against. So a man would be elected with six votes in his favour and two abstentions—but not with one abstention, *and one against*. Which, in Browne-Smith's case, is exactly what happened! Again, in Westerby's case, it's exactly what happened! So you hardly need to be a roaring genuis to come up with the explanation that Westerby had probably voted against Browne-Smith, and Browne-Smith against Westerby. Hence the mutual, simmering hatred of those two senior fellows.

"But let me tell you a very strange thing, Lewis. In fact, you *do* need to be a genius to understand it! Not so much now, of course—but certainly at any earlier point in the case. Let's recap. The first man who went to London was confronted with a ghost from his past—the ghost of cowardice in war. But it was *the wrong ghost* that the Gilbert brothers conjured up that day, because Browne-Smith had nothing whatsoever to do with the death of their younger brother. Then a second man went to London, and you know what I'm going to say, don't you, Lewis? He, too, was confronted with *the wrong ghost* from his own past. Westerby had *not* voted against Browne-Smith—he'd abstained. And, in turn, Westerby learned that Browne-Smith had *not* cast the solitary vote against his own election: he, too, had abstained. Yet *someone* had voted against each of them; and as they spoke together that night in London the blindingly obvious fact must have occurred to them—that it could well have been *the same man* in each case! And if it was, then they knew beyond any reasonable doubt exactly who that man must be!

"So we find a third man going to London to face his own particular ghost—this time *the right ghost*. And soon a man is found in the canal here: a man minus a very distinguished-looking head that was framed with a luxuriant crop of grey hair; a man minus the hands—particularly minus the little finger of his left hand on which he wore the large, onyx dress-ring that he never took off, and which his murderers couldn't remove from his fleshy finger; a man minus one of those flamboyant suits of his that were famed throughout the University; a man, Lewis, who had voted against two of his colleagues in the last election for the Mastership; a man—*the* man—who by his own machination had finally been adopted as a compromise, third-choice candidate, and duly elected *nem. con.*; the man whose own ambition was even greater than that of his other colleagues, and his practical cunning infinitely more so; the same man who at the beginning of the case invited me to try to find out what had happened to Browne-Smith—not because he was worried, but because it was his *duty*—as Head of House! Yes, Lewis! The man we found in the water here was the *Master of Lonsdale*."

CHAPTER
THIRTY-NINE

A *Premature Epilogue*

At the end of the Michaelmas term that followed the events recorded in these chapters, it was no great surprise for Morse (or indeed for anyone) to hear that the man whom Dr. Browne-Smith had once described as "quite a good young man" had been elected to the Mastership of Lonsdale. More of a surprise for Morse was subsequently to receive an invitation to a buffet supper in Lonsdale to celebrate Andrews' election. And, without enthusiasm, he went.

Little was said that night about the tragic past, and Morse mingled amiably enough with the college members and their guests. The food was excellent, the wine plentiful; and Morse was just on his way out, feeling that after all it hadn't been so bad, when an extraordinarily attractive woman came up to him—a woman with vivacious eyes and blonde hair piled up on her head.

"You're Chief Inspector Morse, I think."

He nodded, and she smiled.

"You don't know me, but we spoke on the phone once—only once! I, well, I just thought I'd like to say 'hello,' that's all. I'm the college secretary here." Her left hand went up to her hair to re-align a straying strand—a hand that wore no ring.

"I'm awfully sorry about that! I sometimes get a bit cross, I'm afraid."

"I did notice, yes."

"You've forgiven me?"

"Of course! You're a bit of a genius, aren't you? Your sergeant thinks so, anyway. And some geniuses are a bit—well, sort of unusual, so they tell me."

"I wish I'd spoken to you nicely."

She smiled once again—a little sadly: "I'm glad I've seen you." Then, brightly: "You enjoying yourself?"

"I am now."

For a few seconds their eyes met, and Morse was reminded of some of the great lost days and a face that shone beyond all other faces.

"Would you like some coffee, inspector?"

"Er, no. No thanks."

A tall, gangling, bespectacled man in his mid-thirties had joined them.

"Ah, Anthony! Let me introduce you to Chief Inspector Morse!"

Morse took the man's limp hand, and looked upon him briefly with distaste.

"Anthony's one of the Research Fellows here, and—and we're going to be married next term, aren't we, darling?"

Morse mumbled his congratulations, and after a few minutes announced that he must go. It was still only ten o'clock, and he could spend half an hour with himself in the Mitre. Red wine always made him a little sentimental—and more than a little thirsty.

CHAPTER FORTY

The Final Discovery

The head of Gerardus Mercator (as indeed the whole of Westerby's estate) was bequeathed to the fellows of Lonsdale, and that fine head is still to be seen in an arched recess on the east side of High Table.

And what of that other fine head? It was finally found in the early March of the following year by two twelve-year-old boys playing on a Gravesend rubbish-tip. How the head ever reached such a distant and unlikely site remains a minor mystery; but it posed no other problems. The notes of the pathologist who first examined the skull recorded signs of a massive haemorrhage in the chambers of the upper brain, doubtless caused by the bullet still embedded there. Later forensic tests were to show that this bullet had been fired from a .38 Webley pistol—the make of pistol issued to officers of the Royal Wiltshire Regiment serving in the desert in 1942.

ABOUT THE AUTHOR

COLIN DEXTER is the author of seven Inspector Morse mysteries. A graduate of Cambridge, he lists his hobbies as "reading poetry, drinking good beer and playing bad bridge." But his passion is crossword puzzles and for three years he was the national champion in the *Ximenes* cluewriting competitions. He has won the Silver Dagger award from the Crime Writers' Association twice for *The Dead of Jericho* and *Service of all the Dead*. He lives in England.

Kinsey Millhone is . . .

"The best new private eye."   —The Detroit News

"A tough-cookie with a soft center."   —Newsweek

"A stand-out specimen of the new female operatives."
            —Philadelphia Inquirer

Sue Grafton is . . .

The Shamus and Anthony Award winning creator of Kinsey Millhone and quite simply one of the hottest new mystery writers around.

Bantam is . . .

The proud publisher of Sue Grafton's Kinsey Millhone mysteries:

- ☐ 26563 "A" IS FOR ALIBI $3.50
- ☐ 26061 "B" IS FOR BURGLAR $3.50
- ☐ 26468 "C" IS FOR CORPSE $3.50
- ☐ 27163 "D" IS FOR DEADBEAT $3.50

> "The finest series of detective novels ever written by an American."
> —*The New York Times*

ROSS MACDONALD

PRAISE FOR A GENIUS OF THE GENRE

"It was not just that Ross Macdonald taught us how to write: he did something much more, he taught us how to read, and how to think about life, and, maybe, in some small, but mattering way, how to live. . . . I owe him." —*ROBERT B. PARKER*

"Ross Macdonald's work has consistently nourished me. . . . I have turned to it often to hear what I should like to call the justice of its voice and to be enlightened by its wisdom, delighted by its imagination, and, not incidentally, superbly entertained."—*THOMAS BERGER*

"The most important successor to the Chandler/Hammett tradition, as well as the writer who elevated the hard-boiled private-eye novel to a new 'literary' form." —*MARCIA MULLER*

"[The] American private eye, immortalized by Hammett, refined by Chandler, brought to its zenith by Macdonald." —*The New York Times Book Review*

"A more serious and complex writer than Chandler and Hammett ever were." —*EUDORA WELTY*

LOOK FOR THESE
ROSS MACDONALD MYSTERIES

Special Offer
Buy a Bantam Book
for only 50¢.

Now you can have Bantam's catalog filled with hundreds of titles plus take advantage of our unique and exciting bonus book offer. A special offer which gives you the opportunity to purchase a Bantam book for only 50¢. Here's how!

By ordering any five books at the regular price per order, you can also choose any other single book listed (up to a $5.95 value) for just 50¢. Some restrictions do apply, but for further details why not send for Bantam's catalog of titles today!

Just send us your name and address and we will send you a catalog!